ANOTHER MAN IN THE STREET

ANOTHER MAN IN THE STREET

A NOVEL

CARYL PHILLIPS

FARRAR, STRAUS AND GIROUX   NEW YORK

Farrar, Straus and Giroux
120 Broadway, New York 10271

Printed in the United States of America
First edition, 2025

Library of Congress Cataloging-in-Publication Data
Names: Phillips, Caryl, author.
Title: Another man in the street : a novel / Caryl Phillips.
Description: First edition. | New York : Farrar, Straus and Giroux, 2025. |
Identifiers: LCCN 2024019045 | ISBN 9780374613556 (hardcover)
Subjects: LCGFT: Novels.
Classification: LCC PR9275.S263 P4724 2025 | DDC 823/.914—dc23/
    eng/20240520
LC record available at https://lccn.loc.gov/2024019045

Designed by Abby Kagan

Our books may be purchased in bulk for promotional, educational, or business
use. Please contact your local bookseller or the Macmillan Corporate and
Premium Sales Department at 1-800-221-7945, extension 5442, or by email at
MacmillanSpecialMarkets@macmillan.com.

www.fsgbooks.com
Follow us on social media at @fsgbooks

10 9 8 7 6 5 4 3 2 1

For Lucien and Andre

CONTENTS

ANOTHER MAN IN THE STREET

1 🌱

CALLING THE WORLD

WE WERE SITTING OUT ON DECK listening to the sound of the sea. I say *listening* because it was so dark it was difficult to see the water. The deck lights above our heads were angled so they pooled about our feet. Complementing the sound of the sea, I could hear the low, intrusive grinding of the ship's engines. On the first night it had been impossible for any passengers to sleep, given this constant noise. Furthermore, we were skittish and excitable emigrants, and our heads were populated with thoughts of what lay ahead in England. By the start of the second week most of us had accustomed ourselves to the perpetual rumbling vibration of the banana boat, and the mind-numbing reality of the passage had now effectively stifled our initial enthusiasm.

I was cold, for the night breeze was getting stronger. I was also uncomfortable with the way this arrogant Englishman was talking to me. Once again, the captain laughed, and then he quickly drew his sleeve across his mouth. He leaned forward on the three-legged stool, but kept his head low and his chin tucked into his chest. For a moment, I thought the drunken man was going to topple onto the deck, but he suddenly readjusted his position, sat up straight and continued to speak.

'So, do you know why they call the place St Kitts?' He laughed quietly, but it was mocking laughter. 'Come on, Sonny Jim, didn't they teach you that in school?'

I was tired of this man's questions, but young Billy had insisted that the captain possessed a good heart. Billy claimed he wasn't afraid of the boss man, but after two weeks on the ship I knew that all the crew, including Billy, were wary of this unpredictable bully.

'Yes, I know why they call the island St Kitts', I said. I spoke defiantly. Then I yanked my thin cotton jacket even tighter around my hunched shoulders. In a few days, most of the fellars would be putting on their landing suits so they would look nice and sharp for England, but this jacket was the best I could offer the mother country. I had already decided that England would just have to take me the way I was.

St Kitts was a long way behind us now. I had left both my parents, and two older sisters, in what I was already thinking of as the old world. But I knew that the family wouldn't miss me. They had no ambition, and they all felt safe within the narrow orbit of their predictable island lives. Why should they feel anything for me? After all, I had long ago left them

and gone to live in the room at the back of the piano teacher's
house. It was the only way I was going to get any privacy and
peace and quiet. When I went to find my father at the stables
to tell him that I'd finally saved enough money to buy a passage to England, he looked me up and down and sucked his
teeth dismissively. He made it clear that, as ever, I was bothering him. After all, this was a man who firmly believed you
should bend the tree while it is young, but much to his frustration and disappointment I had never submitted to his
will. Nevertheless, at the end of the day, I walked with the
painfully thin man back in the direction of the village. My
father—a cane cutter who also looked after horses—had very
little in material terms, but he always felt obliged to play the
big man with his only son. He told me that when I reached
England, I must buy an overcoat and a scarf and a pair of
gloves. He insisted, I must do so before winter arrived to bite
me in my arse. I listened, but I wanted to ask this bitter man
why he was talking to me as if he had any experience of England, or any place. The man didn't even own a suitcase, let
alone a passport. He was a country man, working the fields
from sun-up to sun-down during the season, and idling
around, drinking rum, and talking foolishness the rest of the
time. Since I was a child, I had been determined that this
wasn't going to be my life. I had a mind, and I could think. I
sensed that I was different from other boys. I knew, for sure,
that I was not going to emulate my father. Was it wrong to
want to see the world? Was it wrong to want to get away and
become somebody else? From the big pear tree on the bound-
ary of the cricket field, till the dip in the road past the church,
which marked the entrance to the village, my father and I

walked together in silence. There was little point in sharing with my father my hope of maybe getting a newspaper job in England. 'Hope' was a word that was absent from our communal vocabulary, but my girl Lorna understood what I wanted, and she encouraged and pushed me.

'Kitts is short for Christopher', said the captain. He laughed and then continued. 'If you want to be all proper about it, you're from Saint Christopher. You *do* want people to know where you're from, don't you, son?'

Young Billy glanced at me, and then he turned to face the captain. Billy spoke quickly.

'Victor knows that St Kitts is really St Christopher, don't you, Victor?'

The boy's worried eyes darted in my direction, but he didn't give me time to answer.

'St Christopher's the patron saint of travellers, that's what Victor told me. I expect it's all in the Bible. Victor goes to church, a proper English church like us, and they don't have no other languages besides the Queen's English. When he starts gabbing you'll find that he knows some ruddy big words, he does.'

As an anxious Billy continued to speak, the captain sneered and didn't bother to hide his amusement. The man covered his mouth with one hand, while he pushed and prodded with a toothpick. Billy paused and swallowed deeply.

'But *you've* been around the islands, haven't you, sir? I reckon you must know all about their traditions and everything. Next time we dock in the Indies, I'm going to get off the ship and look for myself, instead of just helping with the loading of the cargo. I'd like to see a palm tree up close, and

Victor says they have monkeys on his island. I mean loads of them, that's right, isn't it, Victor?'

An hour ago, it had just been Billy and me out on deck. After dinner, the other emigrants had fallen into the habit of taking a few drinks and playing cards or dominoes. However, as we drew closer to England, I found the short-tempered nature of the men annoying, and their conversation irritating. ('I'm telling you, man, an English pub is a poor man's nightclub.' 'They say you survive one English winter then everything is good after this.' 'It's true, the people don't eat nothing but sprouts and Irish potatoes and cauliflower, and they don't even season the food up or nothing.') To escape the squabbling, I started to come up on deck by myself. I generally sat by the lifeboats and gazed at the stars in the sky. After a few nights, Billy—the boy who worked in the kitchen and served us our food through the hatch—started to come up on deck and join me and, if the wind wasn't too strong, he would smoke a cigarette or two. Although Billy tried to put on a brave face, it was clear the youngster was lonely. He was always keen to turn the conversation in the direction of his 'Essex', a place he habitually described as 'grand' or 'swell'. But, of course, I always used to wonder why, if the place was so 'swell', the boy had left his family and friends and taken off for the sea, but I never put this to him directly. Most nights I was just glad of his presence, especially so as he seemed to understand when to be silent and when to talk. Billy soon confessed that this was his first voyage. I sensed the jittery youth probably wasn't sure how to conduct himself either with us coloureds or his fellow crew members, but I was grateful for his companionship.

Tonight, after a considerable period of hush between Billy and myself, the captain stumbled up on deck carrying a stool. He was a thickset man with a day's growth of beard that never seemed to increase or disappear. To start with, Billy panicked, as though he had been caught out doing something wrong, but as he struggled to formulate a sentence, the grizzled captain sat heavily on his stool, and then produced a bottle of white rum from inside his coat and took a swig. Billy introduced me in a high nervous voice.

'This is Mr Victor, he's one of the passengers.'

The amused captain grinned and then handed me the rum. How, I wondered, did this work? Was I supposed to take a single swig, and then pass the bottle to Billy? I didn't even know if the boy was old enough to take alcohol but, having tipped the bottle to my mouth, I passed it to Billy. As I did so, the captain stabbed a crooked finger in the direction of the stars.

'Do you know how to read the sky?'

I shook my head.

'There's a whole bloody map up there that a mariner needs to understand before he can call himself a *true* man of the sea.'

He snatched the bottle from the boy.

'Billy, lad. Can you read the sky?'

A sheepish Billy shook his head apologetically.

'Don't worry, we'll soon make something of you, my lad. After all, there's fuck all in your Essex worth hanging around for, but these days you could say the same about London.' He turned now and addressed me. 'During the war London was flattened by Hitler's bombs, did you know that?' I shook my head, but the captain missed the beat and pressed on. 'After I got demobbed, I thought I got nobody to go back to so I might as well sign back up with the Navy. This time the Merchant Navy. There's more money and freedom in this line of seafaring. No public school arseholes to answer to, if you know what I mean?'

I didn't know what he meant, but the captain didn't bother to explain.

'At least, after the war, we got rid of that stuck-up toff, Churchill.' He turned now to face Billy. 'But tell me, Billy, why would a strip of a lad like you want to run away to sea?'

'I haven't run away', insisted Billy. 'I got my folks waiting for me. They know I'm coming back.'

The captain started to laugh. 'Oh, you think so, do you? You're married to the sea now, my lad. You can forget Essex.' He turned again and addressed me. 'Like you, the young lad's upped sticks. The poor bleeder's lost, but I've been offering him a little company from time to time. You too? Maybe that's why he's changed his hairstyle, but he now looks like a bit of a spiv, don't you think?'

The captain took another swig from the bottle of rum and stared at me, but I said nothing and just turned my head. That's when the captain started to quiz me about St Kitts, and before too long poor Billy began to talk about monkeys, and then the conceited man fell quiet.

I realized that if I squinted, I could now make out the sea rising and falling like a black undulating blanket. Jesus, I couldn't even remember the last time I'd seen land and I was desperate for this journey to be over. The nonstop irritation of migrant boasting, and the restless lurching of the ship—all of this was feeding my unhappiness. Then there was the nervous anticipation of what lay ahead in England. I was almost twenty-seven and travelling to a place where I hoped to begin again. My job delivering the island's weekly newspaper, *The Labour Spokesman*, had allowed me to save some money, for it had long been clear that buying a ticket for England would be the most sensible way of putting some permanent distance between my father and myself. However, I wasn't prepared to share any of these thoughts with this Englishman. What did this dishevelled captain know of my family or my country? Billy was right. We had monkeys. We also had black sand beaches. We had sugar cane that grew wild and thick like weeds. We had ground provisions and fruit. We had English people looking down their noses at us like we were not fit to walk on the same soil as them. Fuck you, captain, I know all about my St Christopher.

'I'm a bit of a horse man myself', said Billy. 'I've been to Epsom twice, and to Newmarket.' The captain shook himself awake and snickered as Billy continued. 'Mr Victor's father is a groom. He looks after horses on an estate.'

'Is that so?'

'He says they have nearly twenty horses on the estate to do all sorts of hauling and stuff.'

Yes, Billy, but I already told you. We also have a light train that snakes its way through the cane fields. Both the tracks and the locomotive engines come from England. From the industrial heart of the empire. Soon after the trains arrived, they sent out men to instruct us in how to use this equipment, and some of these men stayed on to service the machinery.

Colonial men who during the war chose to idle in the tropics and drink rum, and behave indiscreetly, instead of going back home and fighting for Churchill and England. I've seen these lazy-arse Englishmen.

'But', said Billy, now lowering his voice to a whisper, 'when the trains came, some of the plantations set their horses free in the hills. They let the horses run wild.'

The captain laughed. 'Wild like the people.' He looked at me. 'Are you coming to England hoping to find a white girl, is that it?' As he took another swig from his bottle, I stared directly at the captain, who continued. 'Come on, you can tell me. I know what you coloured boys like to get up to. You're a strapping fellow with needs like everybody else, and a ship is no place for a man to find himself when he's got urges. But don't worry, in England there'll be plenty of lower-class girls for you to caper with. How about you, Billy? You got somebody in mind for your friend?'

Billy laughed nervously, but he would no longer make eye contact with either the captain or myself. The captain passed the bottle to the boy.

'Come on, Billy. I'm only having a bit of fun with your darkie friend.'

Billy made a weak effort to smile, but the captain continued to talk. 'The real worry for us Englishmen is that we're bloody well running out of colonies. India's gone, and some of these ungrateful wretches in Africa have also had enough of us. But you lot need us, don't you? We make things all nice and easy for you, don't we? Cheap passage to England, no questions asked. Sleazy women and lots of jobs. But have you any idea how many of you coloured scroungers are already in England? It's the sixties now and we're still letting you in. We're only a small wee island and we can't take all of you.'

The captain closed his eyes, and then his head snapped forward, but he caught himself. Billy passed me the rum, and once again the poor boy tried to pilot the conversation in another direction.

'Are you looking forward to getting to England?'

I smiled at a distraught Billy, and took a drink. I turned to hand the bottle to the captain, but it appeared that the man was sleeping. Billy continued.

'Once you get to England, you'll be able to ride on a red double-decker bus and see Big Ben and the Tower of London. And don't forget, you're invited to Essex, anytime you like.'

'Billy, I've heard all about the red double-decker buses.'

'And the tube. You've heard of the tube, haven't you?'

I nodded, and then Billy whispered.

'I don't really like rum, I prefer beer. But the captain says there's no more beer on the ship.'

'Billy, I think maybe I should go back downstairs with the others.'

'No', exclaimed the lad, as though frightened at the prospect of being left alone. 'I'm sure the captain won't mind if we finish the bottle. Then you can go down below and join your friends.'

Billy, in St Kitts my father looks after horses. And yes, when the English gave us the gift of a railway, we set most of the horses free. If I close my eyes, I can smell the burnt cane in my nostrils. Before we cut the cane, we burn off the leaves and the smoke obscures the sun. Black flecks rain down from the sky. And then, in the evening, there's laughter at the rum shop. The men sit haphazardly, spilling down the steps and out into the street. But I used to find myself perched alone, a short distance from my father and his friends. After all, I was the strange boy who read books. Detective novels and westerns. Eventually, after sunset, I began meeting up with a girl named Lorna underneath a bridge, and she helped me to find a room of my own. Away from my family. Away from my father. Billy, we had no war. We continue to go to church every Sunday, and we pray to God. We do what you English people want and we stay in our place. But look at us now. We're coming to England, Billy. I've left behind the bicycle on which I used to ride around the island delivering copies of *The Labour Spokesman*. Somewhere down below deck, among all the untidy trunks and boxes, I have a small cardboard suitcase, and I feel nervous but free. Billy, I like to read books and tell stories. There will be no horses in my future. I'm determined to make something of myself. My father—the cane-cutter-cum-groom—he told me that I must buy an overcoat because winter will bite me in my arse. But what the hell does he know? On the day that I told him I was going to England, we walked together into the village. When we reached the rum shop, my father stopped and turned and looked at me. I wanted to tell him about my ambition to write for a newspaper, but the words wouldn't form in my mouth. He laughed and said, I bet you will go to England and be one of those fellars who just play the fool and make a damn spectacle of themselves. That's what my father told me but look at me now. I'm going to England to make something of my coloured arse. Whatever happens, I can't allow myself to fail. The captain started to snore, and Billy suddenly appeared embarrassed. Forget him, Billy. He's just a drunk. I don't want your Essex. I don't need the thrill of a red double-decker bus. I just want a chance to start over without people judging me. But maybe you're too young to understand this?

Beyond the shadow of night, I could still make out the black sea continuing to rise and fall. The captain was now sound asleep on his stool, and Billy's eyes were also beginning to close. Essex, Billy? Why aren't you home in your Essex? And look at me. I'm going to England, not Essex. And I won't allow anything, or anybody, to get in the way of my making a success of my life. I close my eyes. I'm on a ship that is tightly packed with excitable men playing dominoes. But only for a few more days. I think about black flecks of burned cane trash spinning down out of the sky. I think about my mother and two sisters. Have they already forgotten me? Every night, before going to meet Lorna under the bridge, it was my habit to sit outside the rum shop, but slightly apart from the other men, and listen to the static crackle of the one wireless in the whole village. The Englishman would announce, 'This is the BBC calling the world.' And everybody would fall silent and listen. 'This is the BBC calling the world.'

2

IN THE PUB

AS SOON AS THE LAST STRAGGLER had drifted out of the pub into the cold foggy night, we would all make our way to the bar. Once there we climbed onto the stools and waited for young Charlie to pour us a drink and start banging on about having to serve the regulars their pints of 'falling-over water' even though they could see that it was getting close to chucking-out time. We had heard it all before, and as the young lad continued to complain about being so broke that he was having to roll his own dog-ends, and then start bragging about how he'd just learned a new song, or mastered an intricate dance routine, we nodded as though interested. It was then that Charlie announced that in the morning he'd be on his way to the Palladium, where they were holding auditions, and he tried to convince us that this time he was bound to be picked and so we shouldn't be surprised if this was the last we ever saw of him. Our resident fantasist was always adamant that he had a future, and it didn't involve slogging it out in some shithole of a Notting Hill pub where life would inevitably pass him by. However, as usual, the more Charlie talked, the less inclined anybody was to listen to the youngster. We all wanted to tell him, 'Charlie, just pour the drinks and shut your bleeding gob', but nobody ever said anything. We just stared at our glasses and drank until we could feel a little bit of energy seeping back into our tired bodies.

I worked behind the bar with the cheeky little sod, and unlike him I wore a leather apron so I could keep my clothes from getting sopping wet. Before moving to the other side of the bar, I would take off the apron and hang it on a hook by the steps to the cellar, which always amused Charlie. 'Off with your dress, you fucking girl.' Charlie wouldn't be seen dead wearing an apron, and as a result his raggedy shirt and vest reeked, but not wearing an apron was part of Charlie's flamboyant proclamation of transience. Why bother with the costume? He wouldn't be staying. In my own case, I had no reason to imagine that the pub wouldn't constitute my future. I'd been behind the bar for over a year now and I suppose it suited me. The truth is, I wasn't looking for anything else. I'd come from a nothing family in Liverpool that I didn't miss, and London was now my home. I didn't have anywhere else to go. For me, the apron was a sign that I belonged somewhere.

Molly liked to sit next to me, and she made sure that whenever she moved, our knees touched. However, it was done in such a way that if I ever said anything about it, or turned and looked across at her, she could claim it was an accident, and so I said nothing and just swallowed my confusion. To make matters worse, she had also fallen into the habit of running a finger down the side of my face and, in a fake posh voice, suggesting that I ought to take the time to shave properly and show some respect for the job and my appearance. This always made Charlie titter, and the others smile into their drinks. Sometimes, I'd get annoyed inside of myself and wonder if I should just drop a hand down beneath the bar and cop a quick feel of the top of her thigh. But then it would occur to me that because she was waiting for her boyfriend to come into the pub and escort her back to their room, maybe it wasn't possible for her to do anything other than just play with me a little. Perhaps *she* was the really frustrated one.

Anyhow, besides Molly, Charlie, and myself, there was Lucky the handyman, who was seated on the far side of Molly, and the landlord, Mr Wilson, who, once he'd finished in the cellar, would come up and stand behind the bar with Charlie and pull himself a pint of mild. Eventually Molly's fellar would show up. Eamon was an Irish navvy whose thick head was full of dreams. However, the fellar wasn't so stupid that he didn't notice that his girl's affections might easily be cut loose from their moorings and drift in the direction of any passing attraction that took her fancy, hence his rolling up like clockwork every night and joining us all for a drink until his Molly was ready to slide from her stool and onto his arm. Soon enough, they would both depart to a gruff chorus of 'Goodnight, Eamon, goodnight, Molly', and the poor dolt would touch the brim of his cap before holding open the door for her. Once the pair of them had stepped out into the night, Charlie would wait for the nod from Mr Wilson and then top us all up again so we could relax and have one more taste before we were kicked out into the darkness. But on this particular night, Molly's Eamon was late, and Mr Wilson couldn't be bothered to wait and so he tipped Charlie the nod, and once again Molly brushed her knee against my own without a glance in my direction.

It was then that Charlie started to badger Mr Wilson about the need to buy a piano so that the place didn't feel like a funeral home. 'For heaven's sake, Mr Wilson, there's hardly a pub in these parts where the customers don't enjoy a good old sing-song. We're losing punters, or haven't you noticed?' Lucky stood up from his stool and, without making eye contact with anyone, retreated into the back room, where we knew he would set about finishing off his tasks in peace. If ever trouble looked like it was likely to erupt, Lucky wanted no part of it. 'Well?' continued Charlie. 'What do you think about getting a piano?' But Charlie was the only one who couldn't see that Mr Wilson had no intention of purchasing a piano. Finally, Eamon showed up, but he appeared ill-at-ease, and disinclined to take a drink or make small talk with anybody. He simply hurried Molly out of the pub and into the night. Mr Wilson turned from the door and, in an anxious whisper, asked me if he had overstepped the mark with the somewhat unpolished comment he had earlier made to Molly. Seeing her seated on the familiar bar stool right next to me, he'd asked her, 'Molly, has your man jilted you for the night? If so, might an old gentleman like myself be permitted to press his suit?' Molly smiled sweetly in her boss's direction. 'Now then, Mr Wilson, I think you'll find you're a good thirty years beyond what I'm looking for, but my old aunt Bridget has been a widow woman for some time. Would such an association be of any interest to you?' For the briefest of moments, Mr Wilson had looked perplexed, before realizing that he was the butt of a joke. 'Molly McCann, you do understand there's plenty more where you come from, don't you?' Molly had thrust her half-empty glass forward and in the direction of Charlie. 'But you'll not find any with my qualities, Mr Wilson, and I do believe you know this, don't you?'

Having assured Mr Wilson that the exchange was nothing he should worry his head about, I got up from the bar stool. Now that Molly had gone, my plan was to slip into the back room and have a quick word with Lucky before he went off into the night to wherever it was that he lodged. The truth was, I'd never asked him much about himself because the coloured man clearly wasn't the talkative type, so what was the point of putting us both in a tricky spot? I was in my mid-twenties back then, and although I didn't pay much attention to my own future, it was noticeable that now that Labour had won the general election things were looking up. Rationing was long behind us, and we were pretty much out from under the grey shadow of the war. The newspapers were calling it the 'swinging sixties'. Young girls seemed brassier, and their hemlines were going up, while blokes seemed to want to be Mods or Rockers, or just grow moustaches or beards. Apparently, everyone wanted to stand out, and people seemed to be in good spirits and determined to make something of themselves. My one friend from school had left Liverpool and gone off to Canada and, according to the postcard he mailed soon after arriving, he seemed to be doing okay over there. Michael was the only real link I had to the past, but his being across the other side of the Atlantic simply confirmed that I was pretty much alone now. Both my parents were dead, and I'd long ago lost touch with my aunts and cousins and the like, but I imagined that to anybody looking on I probably came across as a genial, carefree kind of bloke. In a few weeks' time it would be Christmas and so maybe young Charlie was right, a piano, or even a television set, might help to liven up the pub a bit, but Mr Wilson tended to hold on to the purse strings like his life depended on it and so it was clear that there would be no cash spent on entertainment in our melancholy pub.

Lucky was up a ladder, but I couldn't tell what he was doing. I shouted but tried to do so without startling him. 'Lucky, what on earth are you still skivvying for? Mr Wilson isn't going to pay you any more.' The coloured man looked down at me with those big eyes of his but said nothing. I shook my head and started to chuckle. 'Isn't it about time you woke up, son, and realized what side your bread's buttered on?' Why I was giving the poor bloke a hard time I'm not sure, but I suppose I didn't like the idea of Mr Wilson taking advantage of him. But why call him, 'son'? We had to be roughly the same age. When I think about it now it embarrasses me that I patronized him in this way. But, as ever, Lucky didn't say anything; he just kept staring, which suddenly confused me, and I completely forgot whatever it was I wanted to ask him. I decided it couldn't have been much, so I tried to lighten the mood. 'Listen, Lucky, just stop this palaver, all right. Come back through and have one more for the road. No need for you to be in here by yourself, okay?'

When we got back to the bar, I was surprised to see Eamon sitting next to Molly, clutching both her hands in his thick paws in a pathetic display of ownership. Clearly, having taken Molly outside to say whatever it was he wanted to say to her, they had decided to step back inside for a drink. Lucky and I sat together, with Eamon's bulk between us and Molly, and we listened to Molly arguing with her suitor about why there was no way she was going with him to America. She wouldn't be setting out for Boston, or Philadelphia, or New York, not any place, for Molly was making it clear that she didn't want to end up as a maid in some posh fucker's home, or worse, on her back in some house of ill repute while Eamon buggered off with the first American slut to cross his path. She'd heard plenty about what could happen to young girls over there with no family to turn to, and she let Eamon know that she was doing just fine for now in Mr Wilson's pub. It was impossible to avoid Molly's raised voice, and while young Charlie stood behind the bar laughing uproariously at Molly's theatrics, a flustered Mr Wilson busied himself with the task of emptying the cash register and stuffing whatever notes he found there into his trouser pockets. I swivelled slightly so I could get a better look at Lucky and whispered, 'As usual, old Wilson is going to lose tonight's takings in some bleeding gambling den. What do you think?' Lucky slowly shook his head but didn't bother to reply as the answer was obvious. It was Mr Wilson's inability to hold on to money that had made me determined not to squander what little I earned on gambling, or women, or drink. Still, I hadn't asked Lucky the real question that had finally come back to me, but I decided that it was now too late to ask him, so it would have to wait.

Initially, I didn't know for sure whether Lucky was from the West Indies, but it seemed logical that a man of his skin colour, and accent, should come from there as opposed to Africa. Growing up in Liverpool, I'd noticed that a lot of the African folks, who tended to congregate by the docks, had scars and markings on their faces. Lucky's face was unblemished. Also, Lucky spoke English that I could understand, which was not the case with the Africans. One morning, Mr Wilson had discovered Lucky standing in the pouring rain on the pavement outside the pub. He invited the bedraggled coloured man to step inside out of the thunderstorm, and I overheard Lucky telling Mr Wilson that he had tried and failed to get office work, but he remembered that a chap on his boat had told him that if he wanted a job in England he should just ask at the Notting Hill pubs. Lucky said that the fellar had told him he had the back for lifting and moving barrels, and that pub work would be better for him as opposed to striving on some factory floor. I watched as Mr Wilson eyed Lucky suspiciously and tried to make up his mind as to what he should do with this sopping wet newcomer. That same night, Molly waited until Lucky was in the cellar before leaning over the bar and whispering to young Charlie that she didn't feel comfortable working with a nigger. For some reason, she didn't look at me. At first, Charlie said nothing. He simply carried on cleaning the glasses with a cloth. Once he'd finished the last one, he put down both glass and cloth and stared hard at Molly. 'You stupid Irish bitch', he hissed. 'That's what people want you to think. That you're better than him. These same people like to behave as though they're better than you. And so it goes. Everybody has a place in the system, except the poor bastard at the bottom. Mr Wilson's got a fucking funny sense of humour calling him "Lucky".'

For some reason, Lucky seemed to like me and he'd occasionally offer up a strange smile, which made me instinctively warm to him. That said, he didn't give much away. At nights, he would sometimes join us at the bar, but most of the time, Lucky appeared reluctant to stick around with us after the pub had closed, and he'd usually leave as soon as he'd finished his tasks. Every so often, Lucky would be back again, his face peering in at the window scanning the pub for young Charlie, who, when he saw him, would grab his coat and hurry out into the night. I once asked Mr Wilson what was going on, but he slowly wiped his hands on his shirt and muttered something about Lucky maybe having to change lodgings, but because I wasn't the kind of fellar to poke my nose into other people's concerns, I just dropped it. On the other hand, Molly never did lower her guard around Lucky, and her eyes would follow him to the door. Then, after the customers had gone, she would simply wait for her idiot, Eamon, to show up. However, she and I both knew that what the little minx was really waiting for was for me to take off my apron, hang it on the hook by the steps to the cellar, and come round and sit up on the stool next to her own so that she might try again to nudge my train of thought onto her track.

In those days, I was a pretty good barman, and the fact that I didn't have any affection for drinking seemed to help. I had grown up in Liverpool with an engine driver for a father who, whenever he could be bothered to come home from the pub, continued to drink whisky like it was going out of fashion. It was then he would raise his hand to my mother, and this kind of behaviour well and truly put me off the booze. By the time I was fifteen, I knew I had to leave home, for my mother wasn't interested in separating from my father, and I'd had enough of getting between the two of them. Accordingly, I packed up all my anger and frustration and did the old Dick Wittington thing and left Liverpool and headed to London. Six years as an apprentice printer taught me everything about the fundamentals of that messy trade, but I soon understood that I didn't want to spend my whole life breathing in poisonous fumes with black ink on my hands. Once my mother sent me the news that her husband had finally taken his last gulp of air in some cesspool of a tavern, I packed it in and went back to Liverpool. And then, after a few years sweating it out on a milk round, and nursing Ma, she too gave up the ghost. Two weeks after the funeral, I came home one day to find that the landlord had put the furniture out on the street, claiming that he'd rented the place to my father, not his sprog. Now that Ma was gone, he'd found another family for the two rooms. With nothing to keep me in Liverpool, I headed back to London and recounted some of this to Mr Wilson when I answered his advertisement for an experienced barman. Of course, I lied and said nothing about delivering milk. I told him that my time in Liverpool nursing Ma had involved me doing pub work, but he looked unconvinced as he muttered, 'Is that so?' Eventually, old Wilson said he'd give me a go, but it was little Charlie the would-be actor who saved my neck, for he could see I didn't know the first thing about serving drinks.

I soon learned that despite always going on about his theatrical ambitions, Charlie had a soft spot for everybody. Charlie, who was barely out of his teens, had been dreaming of a career on the stage since he was a toddler in a Dr Barnardo's home for orphans. Although the lad had enjoyed some sporadic success he was, like many of those in his chosen profession, habitually unemployed. However, Charlie was never resentful. To Mr Wilson's face he was polite, without ever being subservient, but the youngster clearly disapproved of Molly's sharp tongue while secretly, I suspected, admiring her pluck. The frequent eruptions of tension between the two of them were always of Molly's making, for Charlie had the ability to absorb her waspishness without feeling the necessity to engage in any unpleasantness. This served, of course, only to further inflame Irish Molly.

As I got to learn the ropes, Charlie continued to be a great help, and the only moments of awkwardness between us seemed to involve Charlie's opinions on the subject of women. I'd had a girlfriend or two over the years but nothing serious aside from a tenacious seamstress in Liverpool who, during the period of my mother's final illness, conspired to rein me in by freely offering up her charms, which I willingly

accepted. However, the combination of furtive bodily entanglement, once Ma was asleep, and the girl's expectation that I
attend church with her on a Sunday was too complicated a
burden for me to bear. Once I set her aside, the storm of ac-
cusation that was visited on me in the form of banging at the
door, which disturbed both Ma and the neighbours, made me
extremely wary about any kind of involvement with the fairer
sex. At the pub, the odd doe-eyed creature would linger,
usually after a drink too many, and I occasionally squired one
of them back to my room, instead of sitting up on a bar stool
with the others. Charlie never missed a trick, and it was after
one of these nights of hanky-panky that he voiced his matter-
of-fact opinion that women were a source of weakness, and
then he left it. A week or so later, Charlie revisited the subject by announcing that, somewhat improbably, he had once
considered getting wed. Charlie was offering me yet another
conversational path to tread and talk about women, but I
smiled and avoided his anxious eyes, and tried to steer the
conversation back in the direction of Charlie's fluctuating
career as a performer on the stage.

Molly was a tease. I knew that some men used harsher
words to express the same thing, but when squeezed into her
tight blouses and hip-clinging skirts, Molly didn't walk, she
swayed. She did so with pints of beer in both hands and
she always made sure that she bent low to set the drinks on
the table. Of course, in a normal pub you didn't get table
service, but old Wilson thought this gimmick would boost
the pub's takings. Molly did well, and loose change was routinely pressed upon her as a tip, but should a hand touch her
body then she wouldn't hesitate to lash out and slap the face

of the culprit. Should this fail to dampen the offender's drunken ardour then young Charlie or myself were expected to intercede, although it was generally me who stepped out from behind the bar and rescued the situation before it could become any uglier. Once or twice, I felt sorry for the chastised man, for I could clearly see what her game was; Molly knew full well how to walk a thin line between victim and instigator, all the while filling the front pocket of her skirt with coins. What on earth, I wondered, was she was doing with a thick lug like Eamon? His brawn aside, the man lacked the qualities which one imagined might have appealed to a devious girl such as Molly. Every night, I watched the manipulative wench from behind the bar and I knew, without ever admitting it to myself, that I was simply waiting for the right opportunity to press a claim upon her.

One night, when Charlie had left early to catch the last show at the Shepherd's Bush Empire, and Lucky was finishing up in the cellar, Molly cast a quick glance in the direction of the only table at which customers were still slumped, then sidled behind the bar and pushed herself up against me as she pretended to reach for a clean glass. Instinctively, I grabbed her waist and kissed her on the mouth. I felt the wet rag of her tongue thrusting its way between my open lips as she continued to lean hard against me. Then, before either of us had time to acknowledge what was happening, she shoved me away and turned and marched towards the still occupied table, pointing at the clock as she did so. 'Come on, don't you lot have homes to go to?' Lucky appeared and climbed on a bar stool, and in the absence of Charlie waited for me to pour a drink for him. Once Molly had cleared the stragglers out of the pub and bolted the door, she too came to the bar and waited for her drink, which I poured without taking my eyes from her so she would understand. She asked me, 'You ever been to Bristol?' I shook my head. 'My folks left Ireland and set up a haulage business in Bristol, I bet you didn't know that', she said. 'They sure as hell didn't expect me to run off to London and find work in a place like this.' I smiled and asked her, 'What did they expect? That you'd marry the Prince of Wales?' Molly laughed. 'Well, they were hoping for a better class of person than that.' At this, Lucky started to laugh, but Molly cut her eyes in his direction. 'Something amusing you?' Lucky pushed his glass towards me for a refill, which I'd never seen him do when Charlie was behind the bar. I filled him up again and watched as he began to drink in chastened silence.

That night, Molly started to talk about why she didn't much care for Bristol, and I tried to outdo her, describing Liverpool as the type of miserable city in which only a fool would voluntarily remain. And then the conversation turned to where on the face of God's earth we might choose to reside if we were given a free choice. I had no hesitation in declaring myself wedded to America. 'New York City. How could a man not fail to make something of himself in a place like that?' Molly laughed sarcastically, put down her glass, and then raked a hand back through her hair. 'Well, maybe you and my Eamon ought to get acquainted and the pair of you fuckers go off and make a future together.' I knew that Molly had reservations about America, but I had no idea how to respond to such a comment. I quickly declared an interest in Paris, although for the life of me I've no idea why as the city had never before crossed my mind. Molly nodded thought-fully. 'Now, there's an idea', she said. 'A gentleman could turn a lady's head with such a notion.' I looked across at Lucky. 'And what about you, Lucky? You appear to have seen some-thing of the world. Have you some thoughts on the matter?' Again, Lucky pushed his glass across the bar, causing me to raise my eyebrows. 'You sure?' The anxious-looking coloured man clutched the glass with his long fingers. I suggested, 'You'd best make this drink one for the road.' Lucky nod-ded, and once I'd topped him up again, he slowly lifted the glass to his thick lips before replacing the vessel on the countertop.

As I'd hoped, Molly came back with me to my attic room, and we huddled up together in bed against the cold. It wasn't much of a room, with just a narrow bed, a cooking ring set on top of a badly balanced table, a scrap of rug on the bare floorboards, and a window that gave out onto an endless lat-ticework of rooftops. A thin raggedy scrap of sheet served as a hopelessly inadequate curtain, and it didn't fully cover the window, which rattled every time a train roared past. I reck-oned Molly couldn't have been expecting more, and I guessed that her circumstances were probably just as reduced as my own, but we didn't bother with small talk. In the morning we lingered under the coarse khaki blanket until the light at the edges of the sheet suggested it was almost midday and we would soon have to ready ourselves to make an entrance at the pub. We left my room together, but Molly insisted that I go on ahead while she would come along some minutes later and, out of breath, declare that she was late because she had forgotten her bonnet, or some such thing, and had therefore been obliged to dash back home and fetch it. Irish Molly played her part well. 'Sometimes I believe I'd forget my own name if I didn't mind myself.' Young Charlie threw a quick glance in my direction, but I ignored him and began to lay out the clean glasses. I asked him about last night's show at the Shepherd's Bush Empire, and if there was any possibility of his getting an audition with the company, but Charlie responded with a disconsolate shake of the head. Then I watched over his shoulder as Molly fastened on her apron and, carefully carrying a nest of pint glasses on her tray, sashayed over towards some regulars in the corner who sat staring out the window at the snow, which was now falling steadily.

Molly and I soon established a pattern. Each night, we would leave together and hungrily explore each other's body until we fell asleep in a tangle of blanket and limbs. Then, in the late morning, we would make our way back to the pub, although there was no longer any point in arriving separately for it was now clear what was going on, although nobody addressed the new arrangement directly. Initially my questions as to how we might handle the problem of Eamon were met with Molly's dismissive laughter. 'Are you seriously worried about that arsehole?' Whatever it was that Molly did, she definitely took charge of the situation, for the fool Eamon stopped calling for her at the end of an evening. I would sit next to her on a bar stool no longer concerned that I might, at any moment, feel the ominous weight of a hand seizing the collar of my shirt or the booming voice of a spurned suitor asking me if I would care to step outside. Eventually, I relaxed a little, and the pair of us settled into a romance of sorts.

Shortly after Molly and I acknowledged ourselves to be a

couple, a clearly troubled young Charlie decided to leave the pub and set off on a six-month tour of Australia with a comedy variety show. We didn't hear about the tour from Charlie himself, it was Mr Wilson who, one night after we'd locked up, positioned himself behind the bar and draped an arm around Charlie's slender shoulders. He started to make a speech about how determined and focused Charlie had been in his ambitions, although he admitted that he had not always been happy giving Charlie leave to attend his blessed auditions at all times of the day and night. However, old Wilson continued and announced that he was pleased that Charlie had finally got the break he so richly deserved. Charlie began to colour up, for he had not said a word to anyone about his plans, but as we all raised a glass to him, Charlie managed a smile. It was only when Mr Wilson had returned to his office in the back that Charlie began to hurriedly explain the details of his 'break'. 'And so, it's off down under for me, with the kangaroos and convicts, for six months on the old boards.' Molly looked baffled and wanted to know about Charlie's plans for after Australia. 'You'll be coming back, won't you? I mean, for God's sake, you're not planning on making a life for yourself among that scum.' Charlie broke into a little shuffle and then struck an exaggerated pose of the type that I imagined usually punctuated a song-and-dance number. 'Come on, Molly,' he said, 'none of us has a clue what the future might hold.' It was then that a silent Lucky emerged from the cellar, but he failed to say hello or make eye contact with anybody, including Charlie, as he prepared to leave the premises.

For a week or so, I served drinks by myself and wondered

if Mr Wilson would ever get around to hiring somebody to replace young Charlie. I feared not, because for some time now it had been clear that the pub takings were nothing to write home about. One night, the increasingly enigmatic Lucky asked if he might speak privately with me out back, and so I asked Molly to watch over the bar while I stepped into the damp, overcrowded yard that was stacked high with old crates and empty barrels. I stamped my feet to keep out the cold. 'Well, Lucky, what the hell is it? I'm fair freezing to bloody death.' The coloured man lowered his voice and asked if, at the end of the night, I would accompany him back to his lodgings and help out with a problem that was bothering him. I remained mystified and encouraged him to share with me the nature of the problem, but Lucky looked over my shoulder as though we might, at any moment, be discovered. Not wishing to catch my death of cold, I decided to go back inside, but I told Lucky I would see him in a few hours. As I slipped behind the bar, Molly gave me a puzzled look, but because I could sense that Lucky's eyes were still upon me, I quickly whispered, 'I'll tell you later.' An exasperated Molly stared at me and then went about her work. That night, after the last customers had departed the pub, I left a now angry Molly with an unusually talkative Mr Wilson and stepped out into the darkness with Lucky.

I followed Lucky as we wound our way through the murky West London streets, each turn delivering us into even narrower alleyways. Our footsteps echoed against the cobbles and our breath clouded in front of us in shapeless steamy patterns. Finally, Lucky stopped before a flight of worn stone steps that led to a heavy metal door which boasted a dull brass knocker. He pointed to the entrance. 'Maybe you can speak to the man in there about getting back my belongings?' As we had ambled through the night streets, Lucky had slowly explained that the manager of his hostel had recently decided he no longer wished to house any coloureds, and then compounded this insult by telling Lucky that he still owed a week's rent and they'd be holding on to his belongings until Lucky paid up. Fortunately, Lucky had a new place to stay, for now that Charlie had left for Australia, he was able to move into Charlie's bedsit. However, even though Lucky had made it clear that his confiscated possessions amounted to only a few books and some clothes, he insisted he wanted to retrieve his things from the hostel. Ostensibly, this was a matter of principle.

It was a shaven-headed bull of a man who cracked the door to the building. He looked at me with hostility, and then beyond me to Lucky, who was lurking in the semi-gloom at the foot of the steps. The man began to laugh as though amused by our presence. 'Oh, Jesus', he snorted, and then the man asked if I had his money. I shook my head and told the oaf that Lucky couldn't owe rent for a place that didn't want him. I continued: 'We don't want to cause any trouble; we just want my friend's belongings and then we'll be on our way.' I paused and waited for a response, but the man's eyes wandered from my face to the determined figure of Lucky, and then back in my direction. 'You some kind of nigger-lover, then? Is that what this is about?'

The following week, Lucky thanked me again. After some distasteful exchanges, the buffoon at the hostel had reluctantly tossed an old suitcase containing Lucky's things in my direction and told us both to 'fuck off'. But Lucky's thanking me yet again was just a prelude to his admitting that he was once more having accommodation problems. When Charlie's landlady knocked on the door for the rent money and discovered that an immigrant was now living in Charlie's bedsit, Lucky had been immediately slung out. A defiant Lucky had now moved into a dilapidated coloured men's hostel near Lancaster Gate where, according to Lucky, residents were expected to snag a random bed on a rota of first-come, first-sleep. The coloured man's disheartening news simply contributed to an already sorrowful atmosphere in the pub. Sadly, without young Charlie's cheerful prattle, the habitual get-together at the end of the evening was becoming strained, and old Wilson was reluctant to join us as it was clear that money worries were responsible for his remoteness. These days, Molly seemed increasingly uninterested in anything I did or said. Some nights she would hop on a bar stool, have a drink, and then go off to her own lodgings by herself. On other nights, Molly didn't even bother to let me know that she would be leaving without having a drink. The situation was becoming embarrassing. The last thing I needed was people beginning to feel sorry for me, so I suggested to Lucky that it might be a lark to go with him to his coloured hostel and smoke some hemp with his friends. I'd never tried the stuff, but I assumed that's what all the coloureds did as they listened to their music. Lucky looked closely at me, and I could see that he was puzzled. But then he smiled and said, 'Friday'. That was all; just, 'Friday'.

It was nearly midnight as I walked with a silent Lucky along the Bayswater Road, and then down a side street where

I could hear coloured music blasting out of some distant house. I sensed that we were getting close to Lucky's new lodgings, for the number of brown faces on the streets had begun to multiply. Also, I saw the way people were looking at me, wondering what justification I might have for being in this part of town on a Friday night. As we rounded yet another corner, Lucky jabbed his finger in the direction of a large brick building with the name, 'Coloured Hostel', emblazoned in large white letters above the door. It was then that I heard a friendly greeting boom out. 'Victor, you all right, man?' Lucky turned in the direction of a coloured man across the street who was hurrying away from the hostel. 'Wilfred, later, all right?' was Lucky's brief retort, and in this instant, I realized that this was the first time I had ever heard Lucky raise his voice above a melancholic whisper and betray any real animation.

I followed Lucky inside the crummy hostel and could see that damp patches were causing the walls to swell and give off a foul odour, as though somebody had stuffed rotten food behind the plaster. The stench of the place was putrid, and this bug house of a building should undoubtedly have been condemned years ago. I coughed noisily as dust became trapped in my throat, and then I squinted, for my eyes had begun to water. Lucky led the way up a rickety, uncarpeted staircase but, for some reason, all the coloured men looked like they were set on leaving the building. As we slowly climbed the stairs they moved downwards in a seemingly endless stream of what appeared to me to be silent malevolence. Once we reached the second-floor landing, Lucky turned sharply to the right and walked past two closed doors before entering an open doorway where three coloured men sat cross-legged on the floor unmistakably awaiting our arrival. Lucky pointed to me and simply announced my name before encouraging me to also sit on the grubby floor, which was covered in cracked lino whose chequerboard pattern made little sense, for the formerly white squares were now a filthy grey. A single forty-watt bulb dangled from the ceiling, and in the far corner a fume-ridden paraffin heater provided some warmth. Our three hosts had caramel complexions, which suggested that their blood might well be more Arab than West Indian, and they were evidently older than Lucky and me. All three of them eyed me with a severity the origins of which remained a mystery. Meanwhile, Lucky chose to sit at a slight distance from me and the three men, and he seemed to be uninterested in acting as any kind of intermediary. I had effectively been cast aside.

The men began to smoke their hemp, and they included me in the ritual. I watched carefully, then took the pipe and did as they did, sucking in the smoke. Never having smoked before, I expected to feel a rush of new sensations, but I actually felt very little. I dutifully passed the pipe to the man next to me and then felt myself breaking out into a stupid grin that was unreciprocated by anyone in the room. One man pointed to my beard and asked how old I was. I said twenty-six, but foolishly held up two fingers then six as though speaking to a child, and I immediately regretted doing so. Clearly twenty-six was an age that caused them some amusement, for the three men laughed and muttered something to each other, but I had no idea what they were saying. However, whatever it was I could tell that they all regarded my presence in the room as an absurd distraction. I turned and looked at Lucky, who continued to sit cross-legged in the corner. I was hoping for some support, for the atmosphere was becoming increasingly tense, but my coloured friend seemed angry and frustrated. Ten or fifteen minutes later, and without any warning, Lucky suddenly uncrossed his legs and forced himself upright before speaking. 'Thank you for allowing this man to visit with you. I think his evening is now finished.' Lucky looked at the three men, who I assumed also lived in this Coloured Hostel, but they said nothing. Then, as the men continued to smoke their hemp, Lucky offered up a little bow like some bizarre music hall chappie preparing to make an exit, and then began to move towards the open door. Apparently, I was expected to follow.

Once we reached the street, a somewhat surly Lucky asked if I knew my way back to the pub. Obviously, he thought I might be returning there, but it was late, and the place would be locked up. I tried to lighten the atmosphere and assured Lucky that I would be fine, but the coloured man just stared hard at me. 'You better watch that Mr Wilson. I think he likes your Molly.' I now felt a sudden upsurge of indignation that was no doubt fuelled by my exasperation with the manner in which Lucky had been treating me since we had embarked on this adventure. Just what the hell was the matter with Lucky, thinking that he could talk to me like this? I hadn't done him any wrong, so why all this attitude towards me, and now he wanted to drag my girl into it. I'd just about had enough of him lording it over me, and for what? I'd helped him out with his bloody possessions, and been decent enough to him in the pub. I'd treated him like an equal. All

I wanted was to smoke a little hemp and be his pal. Without saying anything more, the coloured man turned and began to make his way back up the stairs of the hostel, but I remained anchored to the street. I was infuriated, for there was no need for him to have behaved so rudely. What he said about Molly was ungenerous, but I was now more immediately preoccupied with how I might make my way out of this neighbourhood, for I could already tell that it would not be a good thing to appear lost in these parts and draw any attention to myself.

That night was the only time I ever tried to make a journey into Lucky's life. Unfortunately, everything about the evening had been a failure, and as I walked back to my room, I thought about what I really expected to achieve by attempting to befriend a coloured man. I was disgruntled, but I couldn't blame anybody except myself for this stupid expedition. It wasn't the hemp that I was seeking, for as it turned out the stuff had precious little effect on me. Somewhere at the back of my mind, I knew that what I was looking for was friendship, but inevitably, after that one night, my relationship with Lucky changed. The following day, the coloured man seemed to go out of his way to avoid contact with me, and there was a mournful aspect about him. Shortly before we closed for the afternoon, Mr Wilson came up from the cellar and took my arm. He steered me out into the backyard. 'What the fuck's the matter with the black fellar? He's got his head stuck in a book and he'll barely talk to me.'

I told Molly about my trip into the coloured 'underworld', as I put it, but she was furious. 'Do you want to get your throat cut by a nigger?' I glared at her, unwilling to dignify that kind of language with an answer. 'Won't you look at yourself? You're so pleased with your stupid self. You grow a beard to prove you're a man, but what is it you want? Have you any idea?' During the following weeks, Molly and I continued to sit together after hours, and sometimes we would even go back to my room, where, jammed up against each other in the cramped bed, all antagonism would be quickly forgotten. However, I could sense Molly continuing to drift away from me, for all she now did was talk about her 'future'. The idea of getting away and starting again was always on Molly's mind, but my own journey from Liverpool to London suggested that I'd already escaped and arrived, and to want more seemed unnecessary. On the nights when Molly chose not to come back with me to my room, I'd watch her talking and laughing with Mr Wilson. However, I tried to dismiss any thoughts that she might be betraying me with the old man. After all, what would a young girl like her want with a lag like Mr Wilson, whose undertaking was failing and whose looks had long ago fled? It didn't make any kind of sense.

It was around this time that I started to drink. I'd never been one for indulging and could always be relied upon to keep my wits about me, but things really started to go downhill when Eamon began to once again show his face at the pub and plonk his big backside down on a stool like nothing had ever happened. I found it unbelievable that Molly didn't even have the decency to talk to me about what was going on with her and this man. No conversation, no confession, no nothing; one minute, Eamon was a distant memory, the next there he was, bold as brass, pushing his glass across the bar for me to refill it like he owned the place. Mr Wilson seemed happy enough to see him, and for a few days I worried that perhaps Mr Wilson was looking to replace me with this lout. However, after a heavy-hearted week of Molly and the idiot cozying up together at the end of the night, Molly suddenly disappeared, and it was Mr Wilson who informed me that the deceitful woman had gone off to Ireland with Eamon and we wouldn't be seeing any more of her. That was it. No goodbyes, no nothing. Her swift disappearance undid me, and the torrent of emotions coursing through my body suggested that I'd maybe been in love with the woman. In those days, I assumed there would always be another girl around the corner if I wanted one, so I probably didn't take Molly seriously enough either in or out of bed. However, once she ran off with Eamon, I would go back to my room at night, where I could still smell her presence in the place. Consequently, drinking seemed to be the only way I had of coming to terms with my loss. Then, a month or so after Molly skedaddled, Mr Wilson received a postcard from the woman, which he shared with me and Lucky. The card announced that Molly was expecting a child, and old Wilson's hangdog expression served only to reignite my suspicions about what exactly had been going on between himself and Molly, which plunged me into an even deeper relationship with the drink.

After Molly's departure, Lucky and Mr Wilson appeared to grow friendlier, so much so that the old man seemed to have anointed Lucky with the unofficial title of his deputy. Of course, all this left me unsure of my own role in the business. For the first time, I began to do what Molly lamented that I was incapable of doing; I turned my thoughts to the future. I tried to remain cordial with Lucky, but I could see that the coloured man now regarded me with a combination of wariness and pity. The more I thought about it, the more I realized that Molly was probably right when she said that I was patronizing Lucky by asking him to take me to a venue where I could smoke hemp. 'By Christ, man, that's like asking an Irishman if the next time he goes out to get pissed up on Guinness, and beat up his wife, he'll take you along. Why the fuck do you assume that Lucky is a hemp-smoking kind of fellar?' I was now drinking whisky in my room in the mornings, thinking that if I got a head start before arriving at the pub, then I would feel less tempted to sneak the odd glass when I thought nobody was looking. And then I started to steal booze from the pub. Instead of buying whisky from the off-licence, I began to conceal half-bottles in my jacket and smuggle them back to my room. At the end of the evening, I would sit by myself and drink and think of Molly and all that I had done wrong and wonder if the best thing might not be to go back to Liverpool, where I belonged. The pub was on its last legs. In fact, fewer and fewer customers bothered to make the effort to cross the threshold, and the place was beginning to smell.

Not long after the night of hemp smoking, Mr Wilson told Lucky that he no longer had to sleep in the coloured men's hostel near Lancaster Gate. He suggested that Lucky could start sleeping in the cellar in exchange for sweeping the floors, and cleaning the windows and scrubbing the tables, duties that Molly used to make an occasional stab at. So now, Lucky essentially lived in the pub, which in part accounted for his growing closeness with Mr Wilson. However, life in the cellar with the odd rat can't have been that pleasant for Lucky, and Mr Wilson eventually let the coloured man stay in a small cupboard of a room above the bar that had previously been an office. One night, as I was getting ready to leave and go back to my room, Lucky purposefully blocked my path. 'Listen', he said as I unhooked my jacket from behind the cellar door, 'I know what you're playing at, and it will only end badly for you.' Lucky looked around, encouraging me to absorb the full desolation of the deserted pub. 'The place is finished. Don't you think it's about time you stop your tomfoolery and start thinking about saving yourself?'

The following day, when I arrived at the pub, I noticed a short, heavy-set, balding man with a cigar sitting on a bar stool talking with Lucky. They both eyed me warily as I walked through the door, and whatever conversation they had been engaged in came to a speedy conclusion. As I began to put on my apron, I thought about asking Lucky, 'Aren't you going to introduce me to your friend?', but I felt certain that Lucky would just ignore my question. I secured my apron by tying the ribbon into a tight bow over my right hip, and as I did so the new man extended a chubby hand. 'Peter Feldman, pleased to make your acquaintance. I'm a friend of Victor's.' Lucky moved away and took up a seat at the farthest end of the bar, encouraging his friend to come and join him. As a result, the fat man excused himself and left the bar stool so the two of them might resume their discussion in a more private setting. After an hour or so, Lucky's friend slowly stood up and began to button his coat, the exchange between the two of them having come to an end. I watched as Lucky followed his guest to the door and then out onto the pavement, where I could see, through the window, that their conversation appeared to have discovered a second wind.

That night, on a street near my rooming house, a coloured man beat me within an inch of my life. I remember catching sight of the man's face and then, if I'm honest, I remember the odour. The man's breath was spicy as he spat out his oaths in tune with his punches. I had a little money, and a bottle of whisky that I had stolen from the pub, both of which he took, and then, as though for good measure, the coloured man kicked me in the stomach and then in my back as he made ready to leave. For over a week, I lay in my room, drifting in and out of sleep. Dreams of Liverpool and Molly were popular and interchangeable, and one morning I was absolutely sure that Molly was waiting for me in Liverpool, and so I dressed with great difficulty as though readying myself to return home. As I eased into my jacket I finally came to my senses. It was then that I realized I was aching for a drink. Having no money, I reached one hand out to the wall to steady myself and then closed my eyes. Jesus, have mercy on my soul, I thought. What a hell of a state I was in.

After nearly a fortnight, I dragged myself back to the pub and discovered Mr Wilson behind the bar, and a solitary customer in the far corner. The place looked pathetic. I explained what had happened, but the old man seemed puzzled as to why I hadn't gone to the police. But to what purpose? Surely Mr Wilson understood that the police would have no interest in trying to chase down a lone coloured man. After all, that's the sum total of the information I would be able to provide—'he was coloured'—and I knew that as far as the police were concerned *all* the coloureds were up to no good.

A resigned Mr Wilson confirmed that shortly after my disappearance, Lucky had also vanished. The old man claimed to have noticed that for some time drink had been leaving the premises, and he was waiting on an opportunity to catch the coloured man red-handed, but the ungrateful swine had run off before he could be held accountable. Mr Wilson had asked around, and he let me know that rumour had it that Lucky had found work collecting rent for a landlord called Feldman, who had an unflattering reputation as a man who cleared houses of legally protected tenants in a particularly brutal manner. 'Mark my words, Lucky is treading on thin ice. And to think I even let the bugger stay in my pub.' When he finished delivering his news, Mr Wilson poured me a drink. He didn't need to say it, but it was obvious that there was no job for me at the pub. The previous month, Churchill had passed away and black ribbon still decorated the mirror behind the bar. It was over. Mr Wilson poured me another drink. 'I heard from Charlie', he said. 'He's not coming back. The little so-and-so has found himself a job as a stage manager at some youth theatre in Sydney. He claims it's all working out for him. He's a good lad, our Charlie. You mark my words, that boy's got stardom stamped on his forehead.'

The following week, I went back to Liverpool, where, for the next year or so, I moved from one unsatisfactory job to another. I laboured first in a blacking factory, then I found employment down by the docks unloading and loading cargo, and then I had a stint selling tickets for the ferry across the river. I did anything to keep myself busy so I wouldn't feel tempted to start up drinking again. I even worked the doors at the Cavern Club, keeping screaming kids in order as they fought to get in to see whatever shaggy-haired band was the flavour of the month. I sometimes lowered my guard and had relations with a willing girl, usually a student or a shop assistant, lasses who knew what the score was. I preferred it that way as there was no danger of getting my heart broken again.

And then I met Betty, who was completely different from all the others. She was a teacher in the Wirral, and early one evening she was walking by the club and decided to pop her head in to see what all the fuss was about. At least she claimed that's what she was doing, but later on she confessed that she'd seen me standing in the lobby and thought I looked both cute and lost. Well, nobody was around, so I offered to give her a little tour of the place so I could get chatting with her. Once the spin around the club was over, I didn't want her to go so I just kept gabbing on like some idiot. I didn't leave any space for Betty to get a word in, but she just smiled and listened as though she understood that I was smitten, and she was therefore going to forgive my bad behaviour. I eventually sat her down on a stool beside me as the teenagers started to pour in for the evening, and she watched as I took their money. Betty popped her feet up on the bar of the stool and dropped her handbag into her lap and held on to it with both hands. Every time I glanced up at her she had this peaceful look on her face as though she understood me, the situation, everything. And well, that did it. I was Betty's, if she'd have me. Finally, I was well and truly over Molly.

I later learned that Molly had a girl, and then she and Eamon decided to make a go of it in Boston, where they had a second child, a boy who was born slow. After that they resolved to have no more. It was Mr Wilson who told me this. I ran into him one day when I was down in London. A teacher friend of Betty's had a spare ticket for the England versus Scotland game at Wembley, and Betty guessed that it might be a rare treat for me to have a day out back in the capital. I was walking down Oxford Street minding my own business when I heard somebody calling my name, and then I saw an old bloke with a walking stick hobbling towards me from one of those Soho side streets that are packed with flash, overpriced clothes shops. Old Wilson took off his spectacles and cleaned them with a handkerchief, like an actor playing a part might do, then he popped them on again. He couldn't believe the sight of me. 'Oh, my word, you look in fine fettle. Happy, even.' The two of us made our way to a cafe and exchanged our news. At that stage, I was thinking about how and when I should propose to Betty. After all, she'd helped me to rediscover myself, and everything about the girl was decent. Mr Wilson beamed as I told him about my stroke of good fortune, and the old man seemed genuinely pleased for me.

That was nearly ten years ago. We've now got Roger, who's almost eight, and six-year-old Sally, and we have our own bed-and-breakfast near the university. However, back then, even though I was confident that things were going to work with Betty, I could never have imagined that life would turn out so well. That afternoon in the dimness of a Soho cafe, I was still trying to imagine a future with the pretty schoolteacher who'd stolen my heart. I listened as Mr Wilson told me that he had sold the pub and he now served behind the bar of a gentlemen's club in the West End. 'Got some airs and graces about the place, the snooty bastards.' But Mr Wilson had no idea about Lucky. 'After the rent-collecting caper with the Jew boy, who knows what became of him. Maybe he got into a bit of bother with the law, but if he did then it's a shame. He had a real brain, that's for sure. He may have been a bit light-fingered, but he wasn't stupid.' Old Wilson paused. 'I suppose it's possible that he just disappeared back to where he came from. Or maybe he followed young Charlie down under.' We both looked through the window and out into the busy West End street where the young dolly birds were bustling about trying to look like Twiggy, while the young men were squeezed into frilly shirts and tight trousers. Suddenly it all looked faintly ridiculous to my eyes, but old Wilson seemed transfixed. Then I looked at my watch and realized what the time was. Although I didn't much care for football, I'd have to get a move on. After all, it *was* England versus Scotland, and I was one of the fortunate ones who was on his way to Wembley. I was excited. 'Do you remember', asked Mr Wilson, 'if I treated him badly?' The old man turned to look at me. 'You know, I've thought about this a lot. I gave him a job, a place to sleep, I was decent to him, but for some reason they don't want to know us, do they? I'm right about this, aren't I? They just don't want to know.'

3

CRICKET, LOVELY CRICKET

VICTOR SIPPED SLOWLY AT HIS BEER, unable to decide if he should have another one. An irritated Claude picked up his empty pint glass and dangled it in front of his colleague's face.

'Man, you drink like a woman.' Claude banged his glass down on the table and sucked his teeth. 'Well, you getting me another drink or you going to play with that thing for the rest of the night?'

Victor understood that Claude was a man who tried to maintain a regular routine. He was always the last to leave the congested office above the fish-and-chip shop, and he seldom lingered beyond six o'clock. The two part-time members of staff left at five o'clock on the dot and hurried their way down the stairs, but as deputy editor, Victor felt obliged to hang around and keep Claude company. He generally busied himself proofreading articles, or chasing down overdue copy, or looking through the pile of books that needed to be reviewed. He knew that Claude liked it when he stayed behind with him, as though his presence affirmed Claude's authority. However, at some point before six o'clock his 'boss' would suggest that the pair of them make their way to the Coach and Horses for a 'quick one', although Claude had no understanding of what a 'quick one' meant.

Victor put down his drink and looked at his editor, who now nudged his empty pint glass in Victor's direction.

'Well, you have holes in your pockets? Or maybe somebody cut off your blasted hands?'

Victor ignored an agitated Claude and thought again about the awkward situation that he now found himself in. When the riots—or youth insurrections, as he preferred to call them—began to die down, his invitations to contribute short items to the BBC, or to the national broadsheets, began to falter. Then they dried up altogether. Victor had welcomed the extra money, and the flattering attention from the media, but the situation had created tension between himself and Claude and made life in the *Race Now* office unpleasant. Some days, Claude barely spoke to him, and when he did, he inevitably made a barbed comment designed to remind Victor that he owed his career to him, for it was Claude who had offered him a path into journalism. The older man was jealous and hurt, for it was obvious that the mainstream press regarded Victor, not Claude, as the West Indian journalist most closely in touch with the anger of the second-generation black kids on the streets, and the man who could best articulate their frustration.

'Victor, you want me to die of thirst? Come on, stand your round.'

Claude lit a new cigarette with the one he had almost finished, then impatiently crushed the old cigarette into the ashtray.

'Claude, man, I'm trying to decide if I want another drink.'

'Who the hell asked if *you* want a drink?'

Victor reached over, picked up Claude's empty pint glass, and got to his feet. Then he lifted his own glass, emptied it, and looked down at Claude. 'Same again, right?'

'You playing for time now? You trying to bat for a draw?'

The landlord had the kind of handlebar moustache that Victor imagined you only saw on people who had served in some branch of the military, most probably the Air Force. But given the slow deliberation with which the man moved, this must have been a long time ago. Victor knew that back then the Coach and Horses would unquestionably have been a strictly white working-class pub, as were most of the others in this part of West London. In fact, a dozen years ago, soon after he arrived in England, Victor had found work in a pub like this one, a dismal place on its last legs. However, as coloured immigrants continued to pour into the country, landlords quickly understood that they could not afford to be too choosy about whom they served. Now the majority of London pubs catered to a mixed clientele, although blacks and whites still tended to drink separately, which always made Victor feel a little uncomfortable. If people worked together then why couldn't they also relax together? The land-lord slid the two pints across the wooden bartop and then wiped his hands on a towel that was tucked into his belt, before opening his palm for the money. As he did so, the bleach-blond barmaid came in through the back door and unfastened her coat, which she then draped over a pile of empty crates. The barmaid smiled as she adopted her familiar stance, with her hips inclined forward like an invitation.

'All right, love?'

Victor smiled back, but he could smell the cigarette smoke that he knew would remain trapped in the woman's clothes and her hair. Why Doreen bothered to go out back to smoke was beyond him—perhaps she liked the privacy, or maybe the landlord didn't like her smoking in his pub—but, whatever the reason, Victor found himself staring intently at her pink Bri-Nylon sweater. He realized that beneath it there was nothing to hold in check her overdevelopment, but he suddenly felt guilty for looking, and so he averted his eyes and remembered his manners.

'I'm doing fine, thanks, Doreen. And yourself?'

'Can't complain.' As usual, Doreen cackled more than she laughed. 'But I will complain if you give me half a chance.'

The landlord handed Victor his change.

'There you go, pal.'

Once Victor sat back down at the table, Claude immedi-ately picked up his pint and sucked the froth off the top. Suddenly his editor had a small creamy moustache, which Claude nimbly licked clear with a slippery movement of his tongue. Having taken a second sip of his beer, Claude re-sumed their conversation.

'Well, I don't know what the fuck you expect me to do, for it seems like you've already made up your mind.'

'Well, I'm asking you for advice, that's all.'

Victor lifted his pint glass to his lips, and as he did so he stared directly at Claude. The man's condescension had, for some weeks now, continued to undermine what remained of their already tentative friendship. Claude was the older man with more experience of both journalism and England, and Victor was grateful to him for having published his early pieces. Back then, Claude's preference was for lighter, more entertainment-orientated articles, but he tolerated Victor's penchant for more dramatic stories about discrimination and prejudice. Victor's job back home, essentially just delivering copies of *The Labour Spokesman*, was no preparation for life as a journalist in England, so Claude had effectively mentored him. Once Victor decided to stop working as a rent collector, Claude offered him a small weekly wage to write for what was then called *West Indian News*. Eventually, the local council provided Claude with funding for a full-time, properly paid staff member, although they insisted that the position had to be advertised. One day after work, Claude sat with Victor in the Coach and Horses and informed him that now that he finally had some backing he was going to relaunch the paper as the slightly more radical *Race Now*, and he invited Victor to take up the soon-to-be-advertised position of deputy editor. When Victor told Ruth the news, she shrugged her shoulders and said that it was about time. Ruth was adamant that Claude was nothing more than a second-rate bully who was totally dependent upon Victor. In fact, to her mind, it was only Victor's energy and commitment that had been keeping the paper afloat, but the older man was never going to give Victor proper credit for his hard work. Appointing Victor deputy editor was all well and good, but Ruth suggested that everybody knew who the real editor was.

'All right,' said Claude, replacing his pint glass on the cardboard beer mat, 'let's be straight with each other. I know all about English people's games. When I come to England I get involved with the communists, and solidarity with the working class and all that kind of thing, but I soon learned that the damn people didn't want to listen to me if I talked race over politics. All they wanted is one or two colonial faces to decorate their socialism, and when Stalin die, and I tell them that the man was a jackarse, they're ready to close me down. The white man's newspaper likes to think of itself as having liberal credentials, but how many black people do they employ? None, right? And why are they interested in you? You think they want you to write about the violence in Northern Ireland, or what it means now that the country has joined the Common Market, or industrial unrest at the British Leyland car factory?'

Victor made ready to respond, but Claude held up his hand. 'No, wait, I'm not finished yet. In America they call it "the black man in the window". Some window dressing, but in essence nothing in the system will change. You'll get more visibility and some more money, and they'll let you write about black issues, and they'll feel good about themselves, and that's it, end of the bloody story.' Claude paused and suddenly his whole demeanour seemed to take on a weary aspect. 'Back home, like an arse, during the war, I walk around in short pants collecting pennies to buy a bomber plane for the RAF.

I believed in Empire Day, and I believed in "There'll always be an England", and so even before I get here England is messing with my head. But I've long since banished that twaddle. I know what I'm dealing with in this country, and it depresses me that these people think that I'm like every other black man and stupid enough to throw away my money on the pools hoping that Littlewoods is going to give me a big payout in exchange for ten draws. Victor, man, sometimes I just get tired of this place, and it upsets me to see what it's done to our lives. You understand what I'm saying?'

Victor watched Claude's face cloud over with sadness, and he wanted to lean across the table and drop a comforting hand on his editor's shoulder. He didn't like the way Claude regularly condescended to him, nor did he appreciate his behaviour towards the two office part-timers. There was no need for these fitful outbursts of dictatorial disdain, for they served only to affirm that Claude's time in England had corroded whatever generosity he might have once possessed and transformed him into a tired and irritable man.

'You know, I have credentials for Lords', said Claude, suddenly changing the direction of their conversation. 'Maybe I can get you a ground entrance and we can meet up inside?'

Victor took a drink and then swallowed deeply. 'Are you still thinking of doing a feature on Viv Richards?'

'I'm still waiting to hear from the West Indies press office to see if I can get access to the man himself, but I imagine he has all kinds of responsibilities on his time.' Claude paused. 'You think the youths are going to behave themselves?' And then Claude caught himself. 'Jesus, I sound like the white

man, worried that these young black hooligans might mash
up the sacred home of cricket.'

'I don't think there will be any trouble.'

'Well, if there is I'm sure your new friends will want you
to write about it. After all, it's better if they get a coloured
man to bad-talk the youths so that nobody can accuse them
of racism. I can see the headline now. "Will Lord's Survive
the Black Onslaught?" Claude laughed. 'If you write it, then
it's no problem for them.'

Victor lifted his beer to his lips, but he wished now that
he had not agreed to accompany Claude to the pub, for his
editor appeared to be in a particularly hostile mood. He
looked beyond Claude and stared at Doreen, who was reaching for a bottle of gin from a shelf above the bar. She wasn't
watching him, but Victor concentrated hard so that as soon
as her eyes turned in his direction, he would be able to
quickly look away. However, he suddenly became aware that
the landlord was scrutinizing him, and, without meeting the
man's eyes, he returned his attention to Claude.

'Listen, man, I have to go now. I'm sorry.'

Claude started to laugh. 'You rushing back to Ruth? You
two suddenly discovered something to talk about?'

For a moment, Victor felt himself rising to the bait. Claude
had never made any secret of the fact that he didn't care for
Ruth, but the source of his discomfort with her was constantly
subject to change. Some days, his problem with Ruth was
that she had been disloyal to the man she used to live with,
and so she was clearly not trustworthy. On other days, Claude
would contend that she had no formal training in anything

beyond typing up letters and filing, so what possible use could Ruth be to an ambitious coloured man? Claude was forever implying that the only thing that his deputy editor and Ruth might have in common was sex, and he would occasionally ask Victor if he wanted people to think of him as the type of black man who comes to England and strictly troubles white women, as though they were imperial monuments to be conquered? Victor stared hard at Claude, unsure how to handle his mean-spirited comment about what he and Ruth might, or might not, talk about. Claude smirked, and it was clear that today, his editor was once again determined to let Victor know exactly what he thought of Ruth. 'Victor, my brother, being with a woman like that makes you come across as less than what you are.' Claude paused theatrically and then continued. 'Man, you breed a good coloured woman, and get a son, but you choose instead to take up with Ruth? I mean, if it's a white woman that you want, then trust me, you could have done better than that.'

Victor took one final sip of his pint before climbing to his feet. He pulled on his jacket and then straightened his collar. It was time to leave Claude, probably for good, and take himself home to Ruth. She had his back, and unlike Lorna she wasn't angry with him. He would leave Claude in the Coach and Horses, and leave blond Doreen behind the bar, and leave the landlord with the handlebar moustache who he knew would most likely still be staring at him, and on Monday he would let the broadsheet newspaper know that he was happy to take up their offer and start working for them. Victor extended his hand towards Claude, who laughed as he took it, and then engineered his deputy editor's wrist through the gymnastics of a soul shake.

'Be well, Victor. Walk good, my brother.'

IT WAS ONE OF THOSE HOT SUMMER NIGHTS when every-body in West London seemed to be living out on the streets. Young, excited kids were running wild as though they had no homes to go to, while clusters of men were congregated on street corners, and women were sitting out on steps or talking across garden fences. It had been hot like this for weeks now, and this was definitely the warmest summer that he could remember since he had arrived in England. Victor winced at the stupidity of choosing to wear a jacket, so he slipped it off, looped a finger through the hook, and tossed it over his shoulder. He didn't have far to go to reach back home, so he decided to walk and try to clear his mind of Claude's caustic words. Crossing the road in front of the tube station, he no-ticed a group of youths playing the fool, so that those enter-ing or exiting the station had to run a gauntlet of unwanted comments. Across the road, as though anticipating trouble, a van full of policemen in riot gear was conspicuously present, and the eyes of the officers were trained on the youths. The youngsters could see the police, and from time to time they flicked the officers a two-fingered salute and, predictably enough, received the same in return.

All the way down the main street, the scene was the same. England during the hottest summer on record. Too hot to go to sleep, but if you decided that you wanted to rest then the quake of reggae music blasting from the huge boom boxes would cause your insides to convulse and prevent you from nodding off until the small hours. Just beyond the first junction Victor smelled weed, and then he saw two Rasta guys on a short flight of stairs making eye contact with him and tossing their heads, clearly 'asking' if he needed anything. Victor looked directly at them but kept walking, and then he suddenly worried that he had somehow let them down and maybe they just wanted to talk. He stopped and turned, and slowly made his way back in their direction. The one sitting down, and openly rolling the weed into a Rizla, didn't look up, but he spoke first.

'We can fix you up with something?'

The second man threw a cigarette to the ground, and without taking his eyes from their 'visitor' he stubbed it out with the tip of his training shoe.

Victor spoke quietly. 'I don't need any weed, thanks.'

The first man looked up from his Rizla.

'Then what the fuck you doing here? Me don't know you.'

Victor looked closely at them both. He imagined they thought that their dreadlocks, and their shades, and the drugs, gave them an aura of fearlessness, but their bravado didn't impress him. However, he couldn't argue; it was a good question. He didn't use drugs, so what the fuck was he doing standing in front of two young men who were minding their own business? Smoking or selling weed was a criminal activity, but he wasn't a policeman, and he wasn't their father. As he thought about how to move the conversation along, a young woman in a halter top, and with short braids, opened the ground-floor window and poked out her head. She didn't say anything, but she looked at Victor with the same kind of dismissive pity that Claude habitually bestowed upon him. Rizla man turned to her.

'Lurlette, go back inside, girl. We can deal with this.'

But the young woman didn't go back inside.

'Hey, old man', she shouted. 'Where you get those shoes? Jesus Christ, somebody tell you that brown lace-up shoes is in fashion?'

Both the man standing at the top of the stairs and the young woman started to laugh, while Rizla man casually rolled his joint to completion and lit it. The young dread took the first hit as his friends continued to laugh. Victor watched the youngster trap the smoke in his lungs, close his eyes, and then totally unexpectedly the Rasta youth held out the joint for Victor to take.

'Thanks, but I better go.' Victor wanted to say something more, but he had been totally wrong-footed by this gesture, and he suddenly felt out of his depth with these people. 'Take it easy' was all he could think of to say, before following it up with a somewhat insipid 'You all have a good night.'

As he turned to leave, Rizla man started to cough and then he burst into loud, uncontrollable laughter. Victor hurried away, but he could still hear the man's laughter and the clicking of his brown shoes against the pavement. Once he was sure that he was out of sight, Victor started to run.

Eventually, he stopped by a bus stop and sat heavily on a bench. The armpits of his shirt were now stained with sweat, and he felt wet and uncomfortable. Victor reached one hand behind his back and pulled the damp cloth away from his skin. At first, he had jogged steadily, but he soon realized that he was sprinting, as though trying to escape from danger. As he slowed down and caught his breath, Victor understood that what he was actually running from were Claude's words. Tonight, Claude's taunting had crossed a line. He had been open with the older man about the fact that he had a firm offer of a job on a broadsheet newspaper that would enable him to move on from *Race Now*. Victor had also made it clear that he was grateful for Claude's support across the years, but his acerbic editor had continued to belittle him by suggesting that he had no grasp of the hypocritical realities of English life. Did Claude really think he was so stupid that he didn't understand that part of his value to the media, as either a 'stringer' or a full-time employee, was as 'window dressing'? This was the nature of the game. After all, didn't the local council fund *Race Now* as a form of window dressing? The whole thing was a hustle. 'Race Poli-tricks' was what Claude called it.

A number 28 bus slowed down as it approached the bus stop. Victor stood up from the bench and reached into his pocket for some change. There was a seat downstairs right at the back, and he slid in next to the window and tried to banish Claude from his mind. At the far end of the back seat, he could see a middle-aged woman in a nurse's uniform who was slightly overweight, and whose grey hair suggested she had prematurely aged. Her head was resting against the vibrating glass, but incredibly enough, despite the rattling of the window and lurching of the bus, the woman appeared to have somehow managed to fall asleep. A long shift? A long shift in England? Victor stared openly at her and wanted to ask the woman how long she had been in the country. In fact, why the hell had she left her island and come to England in the first place? Not for the weather. This was the first decent summer they'd had, and the youths were managing to make a mess of that for everybody. Did she ever think about going home, he wondered? Or had she resigned herself to twelve-hour shift after twelve-hour shift looking after sick English people, and then submitting to a long bus ride home, and to what? An ungrateful husband? A house full of noisy kids? What on earth had happened to this poor woman's dreams? It looked like England had broken the woman's confidence. Victor understood that England could do this to you and make you want to disappear inside yourself. But what had England done to his life? And that of his wife and son? Now that he had finally made up his mind to leave Lorna and her nagging, and her oddly eccentric and negligent appearance, and commit himself to being with Ruth, he felt overwhelmed with guilt. Giving Lorna money was the right thing to do, but he knew it was never going to be enough. No wonder his son didn't seem to want to speak with him. Ruth seldom mentioned the 'other woman' or Leon, but from time to time he found himself looking at Ruth and wondering what value she saw in him. She'd forgiven him his deceit, but did he deserve to be forgiven? However, this concern didn't represent the full extent of his anxiety. He was nearly forty now, and a long way from home, and to some extent dependent upon Ruth. Despite the opportunity of this new job, he still found himself troubled by the question of just what had happened to *his* life in England?

Victor got off at the stop beyond his own, having decided to walk the few hundred yards back to the house so he might gather himself. What was wrong with his shoes? Nobody had ever made a comment about his shoes before. Ruth had never said anything about his shoes. His shirt was still damp and sticking to his body, and he felt uncomfortable in himself, but once he got in the house, he would take a bath and wash the day off. As he turned into his crescent, he realized he was following a boy who was carrying a long, bandy twig with which he would whack the trees as though punishing them. On either side of Victor, the scene was a familiar one. People were clustered in the street or sitting out on their steps; windows were thrown wide open, and reggae music floated in the air. Something was going to happen in this country, he could feel it. However, as he stopped in front of Ruth's house, he had no idea of what that *something* might be. In the meantime, once inside, he would give Ruth the good news. He was leaving *Race Now*. Tomorrow, he would not be going into the office above the fish-and-chip shop. Instead, he would stay home with Ruth. And on Saturday, he wouldn't bother meeting up with Claude at Lord's to watch cricket. Next week, he would inform the broadsheet newspaper that he was prepared to sit in the metaphorical window for them. He had not come to England to be a woman sleeping on a number 28 bus. That's what his father expected him to achieve. Nothing. But Victor was not going to allow this to happen. He understood that everything he'd been doing for the past dozen or so years in England had been a kind of preparation for where his life was now delicately poised, and it was Ruth, not Lorna, who had helped him reach this place. And it would be Ruth, not Lorna, who would be standing by his side as he navigated this junction and continued with his journey.

4 🌿

ANOTHER MAN IN THE STREET

RUTH NERVOUSLY FINGERS BACK the net curtain and looks down into the street. He's not there. This Charlie must have something else to do this morning, but he'll be back again, parking himself on the corner and waiting for Victor and, if he doesn't see him, trying to catch her eyes. There is no real buffer between Ruth and the nuisance of this man's presence, for these houses open up right onto the pavement. Where you might expect a small garden with some bushes and flowers, all you get is a couple of dustbins stuffed behind an iron rail fence and a squeaky gate that won't latch properly. Sometimes whole weeks go by, and Ruth doesn't have to deal with this scruffily dressed, decrepit man with thick, unwashed hair and dirty fingernails. Then the crazy man shows up again at the oddest times, and simply stares as she leaves or comes back. He reminds her of the type of men who hang around school playgrounds with their hands shoved deep in the pockets of their trench coats, watching girls come and go. They've reported him to the police and so he's had his warnings. As a result, he knows better than to say anything, but the way he looks at her makes Ruth want to slap his face. Shortly before Victor went into hospital, she once again complained about this Charlie, but Victor simply shrugged his shoulders. 'Look, he's just a dumb out-of-work actor. People get all kinds of shit in their heads, but he isn't going to do anything.' After this dismissive response, Ruth stopped mentioning Charlie. These days, because Victor is in hospital, she must deal with Charlie's irregular appearances by herself, but this morning he is nowhere to be seen and so she lets go of the curtain and watches it flutter back into place.

At sixty-five, she is no longer a young woman. Ruth looks at her face in the small handheld mirror and searches for what? To a generous observer the lines might suggest wisdom, but nothing about her present situation makes Ruth feel in the slightest bit smart. Clearly, she has made a complete mess of everything, and she continues to struggle with the question of whether she should turn in the direction of her past and try to repair some of the damage she has unwittingly visited on others, or simply press on with her joyless day-to-day existence. She imagines that Victor has no idea about her unhappiness. In many respects, he has always been a selfish man, principally caught up with how he appears to others, and it has gradually dawned on her that he has most likely always seen her role as little more than support and helper. Now that he is in hospital, all pretense that she might be something other than this has disappeared. His pulmonary illness, and subsequent chronic shortage of breath, has not resulted in any whispered words of gratitude for her care and attention. As ever, Victor simply expects her to be there for him, but Ruth has recently begun to torment herself with the question of just what on earth she might do to make life more tolerable.

She stares at her unsightly wrinkles, that could probably have been dealt with had she begun a regime of applying cream at an earlier stage. But back then, she naively thought she might always be pretty enough to get men to look at her with some interest. Not that she was a flirt; far from it, but a part of her knew that she didn't have to try too hard to attract scrutiny from the opposite sex. Now she lives with a heavily creased, and decidedly unfetching, face which each morning stares blankly at her and quietly suggests, 'Ruth, love, some more sleep last night might have been useful.' She can't remember the last time she managed more than four or five hours of anxious tossing and turning, before switching on the bedside radio and listening to the early morning bulletins on the local BBC station. However, she only half-listens, for she has little interest in regional gossip, and no desire to change stations and tune in to the predictable babble of national news. Ruth cares not a jot about plans for the upcoming London Olympics, climate change, or trading agreements with formerly hostile countries. As far as she is concerned, none of this affects her, and it never has. Christ, who expects a secretary to have any interest in current affairs? Once she stopped working and decided to do as Victor suggested and carry out some research for him down at the borough library, she had a touch more time on her hands, but she still had no desire to waste her energy keeping up with the shenanigans of politicians or tracking the ebb and flow of the stock market. She would far rather settle down on the plush, but now somewhat tatty, beige settee, with a slice of cake and a cup of tea, and watch television, although she could always tell, by the way that Victor looked at her, that he was often frustrated by her indolence.

Most mornings, Ruth finds herself twiddling the Bakelite knob on the front of the old-fashioned radio and searching for something other than the news. The correct word might be 'company', but to think of herself as a woman who craves companionship makes her feel defeated. Soon Ruth will have to attend to her face and then get dressed and go downstairs, for this morning she will once again return to the hospital and sit quietly with Victor. Through the window she sees the thick, heavy branches of the oak tree across the street slowly swaying in the breeze. The buds will soon be leaves, and Ruth can't wait for the warmth of summer to arrive. And then a thought that periodically troubles her creeps once more into her mind, and she wonders if Victor will ever come home to this house? Ruth replaces the handheld mirror on the side table and moves slowly to the bathroom. She carefully applies some lipstick and then purses her lips. Ruth pulls a tissue from the cube of a box and dabs at the corners of her mouth. Jesus, her nails are chipped, but sod it. Nothing she can do about this now. There is not enough time. She takes a deep breath and tosses the used tissue into the rubbish bin, before tucking a stray piece of grey hair behind an ear. If not today, then at some point soon, Victor will be coming home, and they will resume the life they have made together. Once already, after Ruth discovered the truth of Victor's marital status, they have had to begin things anew after a period of what Victor liked to call adversity. To her mind, Victor's hospitalization might well be regarded as another period of adversity. However, to have allowed her life to be reduced to simply overcoming one bout of adversity after another, and worrying about how she might repair past mistakes, causes her to feel almost permanently unhappy. Ruth gropes for the banister and makes her way downstairs to the kitchen, where she puts on the kettle. A quick cup of coffee while she stands at the Formica-topped counter, and then she will make the short dash to the end of the street and line up for the seven o'clock bus alongside office workers and teachers; people who, given the emotional turbulence of her own world, appear to have enviably mundane routines to their lives.

Last night, her daughter shook her head, before quickly tossing back her large glass of gin and tonic. She then told Ruth that after five or six hours bickering with her, she had reached the conclusion that it was pointless to continue talking. As a result, Lucy had decided to take the late train back north to her husband and twin boys. It was a depressing end to her daughter's short visit. Yesterday afternoon, while Ruth was getting ready to make her second trip of the day to see Victor at the hospital, she heard the unexpected knock on the door. When she took the chain off and opened up, she saw her agitated daughter standing before her. Trying hard to disguise her surprise, Ruth cheerfully ushered Lucy into the kitchen knowing full well that her child must, like her, be fed up with their frustrating phone conversations, which generally ended with Lucy suddenly pressing the 'off' button on her mobile, or her mother putting down the receiver. She could see on her daughter's determined face that Lucy must have decided to journey down to London to have yet another go at talking some sense into her mother—this time, in person.

It was just over a year since she had last seen Lucy. Her daughter had planned a shopping trip to London for the sales, and at the last minute had called and suggested that before heading back home she might have time for a coffee in a place near King's Cross. As Ruth stood and waited for the barista chap to make the drinks, she glanced at her seated daughter, who for some reason had cropped her hair short like a toilet brush, and who appeared as though she could afford to lose a few rolls of fat. It was not a good look for a woman in her late forties, and the tight slacks were not helping, but as Ruth carefully carried the lattes back to their table in the far corner, she knew that she was not in a position to say anything. Now, a year later, Lucy was sitting in her kitchen, and she could see that her daughter's hair had grown out a little, and her proper shape was returning. Ruth filled the kettle and accepted that she would most likely not be going back to the hospital this afternoon. Instead, she would try to listen politely to Lucy, for she had no desire to further damage their already uneasy relationship. Their recent exchanges on the telephone had left Ruth in no doubt that Victor's illness had not resulted in any thawing of the frostiness that Lucy felt towards him. In fact, during the past few weeks, Ruth had been forced to endure her daughter's increasingly impassioned pleas that she start facing up to things and leave the 'arsehole'. As she looked at Lucy seated upright at the kitchen table, Ruth could see a new conviction on her daughter's stern face. She handed Lucy a cup of tea, and a glass of tap water, and then sat opposite her.

'You know,' began Lucy, 'I wouldn't be here if that fucker wasn't still in the hospital.'

Ruth sighed. 'This is his house too, Lucy. I don't think you should be talking about Victor like this.'

'It's shameful. He's a bloody liar, and he's dragged you down to his level, hasn't he?'

'Is this why you won't let me see my grandchildren?'

'Well, can you blame me? I don't want my kids involved.' Lucy paused and shook her head. 'I mean, look at the state of you—you're not an old lady, but it's like you've given up.' Her daughter's voice was becoming strident, so Ruth picked up Lucy's glass of water, drank some, and then went to the kitchen sink and refilled it from the tap. She then sat back down, placed the glass on the table, and watched as her only child picked it up and took a sip. Ruth wondered what else Lucy might have on her mind. Some kind of ultimatum? After all, it made no sense that her daughter would have travelled all the way to London to simply continue to berate her about Victor. Lucy held on to the glass of water but said nothing; Ruth sighed and tried to instill some calm into the conversation.

'I don't suppose you want me to tell you how he's been doing?'

Her daughter looked up at her, and then back down at the glass of water that was now cupped between both hands.

'You're fucking kidding, right?'

The silence deepened. Ruth began to search for another topic, but her daughter spoke first.

'You know . . .' Lucy paused. Ruth looked directly at her daughter but said nothing. 'You're not even a little bit ashamed of yourself, are you? I mean, it's the twenty-first century. Women don't have to put up with this kind of shit, you know. I've had to live with the shame of your not being around for nearly all of my life, and then when I find you—' Lucy suddenly stopped. 'I'm sorry, I don't know what's the matter with you.' Again, Lucy paused. 'I just don't get it. What about my birth dad? Paul. Why did you leave him? The twins get on with him fine, and he told me he wouldn't mind seeing you again. He's a nice guy, so why dump him? Don't you want to see him again?' Ruth offered her daughter a despondent smile. Had Lucy really come to London to just try to hurt her? Lucy pressed on. 'And what about the poor foreign bloke you told me you chucked to go off with this prick? You chose a bullshit artist over a nice fellar with some money in his pockets. And don't look at me like that. It's you who told me the foreign guy was a decent bloke, so what was that all about, then? He was too old for you, you said, and you didn't love him. Well, you don't *have* to be with a bloke, you know. You could have left the foreign man and just been on your own. I mean, were you that desperate?' Ruth looked at her daughter and wanted to protest that she had never been desperate for a man, but she was no longer sure if this was the truth. What she was sure about was that it all seemed to happen quickly, and she somehow ended up exchanging Peter's silence for Victor's lies, and Lucy was right, her behaviour was undignified. But what the hell did her daughter expect her to do now? Lucy began to sneer. 'It's like you've made a real dog's dinner of your life, haven't you?' Her daughter didn't wait for an answer. 'Well, do you want to see my birth dad again?' Ruth looked closely at Lucy, and for a moment she wanted to remind her child that, contrary to what she seemed to believe, her mother's life had not begun on the day that Lucy was born. What she required from Lucy was patience, compassion even, but as she stared into her daughter's angry face she understood that now was not the time to be asking for this kind of consideration.

A few hours later, Ruth watched as Lucy poured a second large glass of gin and tonic and then plonked herself back down on the settee. Ruth had suggested that the cluttered living-room might be more comfortable than the kitchen, but she felt self-conscious, for her daughter could now see her bare legs, and her shoes that were permanently scuffed, and it must have been painfully clear to Lucy that all was not well with her mother on any level.

'Look,' sputtered Lucy, 'you've got to start putting yourself first. He lied to you. That's what he does. He just lies.'

Ruth could see that her daughter was drinking too much, but Lucy had long ago confessed to her mother that she had a weakness for the bottle. Her daughter liked to laugh and claim that it was a genetic problem, one that she had inherited from the family who adopted her, but Ruth understood that this 'joke' was designed to upset her and so she never rose to it. However, if occasionally overdoing it with her drinking was the only mistake that her daughter made in her life, then there was little for Ruth to worry about. She stared closely at her child and wondered if Lucy would ever truly forgive her for giving her up for adoption. Do children ever get over such abandonment? Honestly, sweetheart, if you want to go, then go. Finish your gin and tonic and take the train back to your nice husband and your twins. I understand. But Ruth said nothing, and Lucy continued to sip at her drink, and Ruth's mind drifted.

Yesterday, Victor had not opened his eyes at all. It was one of those frustrating days, and the cranky Polish nurse, who last week offered to help her find Peter, told Ruth that she looked like she needed some sleep. Danuta insisted that there was no reason for Ruth to come back to the hospital until she'd had some proper rest, and Danuta promised that if there was any change in Victor's condition then she would call. A relieved Ruth had returned home with the aim of taking a nap, but shortly thereafter she heard knocking and so she inched her way down the stairs and opened the door and discovered her daughter glaring judgmentally at her. Again, she looked at Lucy, who was fully reclined on the settee with her feet tucked up. Her daughter took another large sip of gin and tonic before lifting her eyes and staring pitifully in her mother's direction. Seriously, Lucy, please stop looking at me like I'm something the cat dragged in. I'm your mother, and you're in my house. It might not be much of a house, and I've clearly not been much of a mother, but I'm trying. Really, I am.

'You know, you're welcome to stay the night.'

Lucy smiled weakly, then shook her head and downed her drink. 'I know.' She stood up. 'But I've got to get back to Matthew and the twins. When you're ready you can let me know about my birth dad. He really *would* like to see you again.'

Ruth hears the kettle beginning to boil and she shakes herself out of her reverie. At just after two o'clock in the morning, Lucy had texted to let her know that she was back home safe and sound. At least there was that gesture. But it pained Ruth to consider that it was unlikely that Lucy was ever going to let her be a grandmother to the two boys. Glancing at the clock on the microwave, Ruth can see that she still has a few minutes to have her coffee and then get to the end of the street in time for the seven o'clock bus. She pours the water on the granules, quickly stirs, then discards the spoon into the sink with a loud clatter. Ruth moves to the window and once again peers out. He's not there, but really, what does this idiot Charlie want? To spit in Victor's face? To be given money? Or maybe this bothersome man simply wants the same thing from Victor that she does: a proper explanation. Anything but the unnecessary affront of silence.

VICTOR WALKED BY PETER'S SIDE and quickly picked up the routine. A knock on the door; a polite 'Good morning' or 'Good afternoon', however discourteous the scowl that might greet them, and then an enquiry as to whether or not they had the rent money to hand. Surprisingly, few people betrayed hostility, and those who did were mainly elderly English tenants who resented the rising tide of coloured people in their midst. They understood that soon they would not be able to afford Peter Feldman's escalating rent, and they would have little choice but to leave their homes. Once these houses

were subdivided into flats, and rented out to desperate immigrants, they would generate far more income. However,
while they remained in his properties, Peter was always scru-
pulously polite to his tenants and simply waited for them to
hand over their money. 'Toodle-oo. See you next week. Be
safe.' Having offered them a Tommy Steele smile he would
press on to the next house. Victor knew that he would never
be able to perform like Peter. He also realized that none of
the tenants, white or coloured, would tolerate him in the way
they did Peter, and he would have to develop his own, more
stern-faced, approach to this business of rent-collecting.

Victor understood that if his father could see him, he
would not approve of his son bullying people in this manner.
At the end of a long day of work, either in the fields or at the
stables, Victor's stick-thin father would wind his slow way
along the road that snaked back in the direction of the village.
He would always stop at the rum shop, where he liked to
settle down on the steps of the shabby building and take a
shot or two, and chat nonsense, till night fell and the BBC
news crackled to life on the one wireless in the village. When
it did, all the men would stop their chatter and bow their
heads and listen. And then, once the news was finished, his
father would stand and begin to shuffle his way into the heart
of the village and return to the two-room house he presided
over. When he arrived home, his father would expect his plate
of food to be ready and his wife and three children to have
waited for him before beginning to eat. And then later, after
dinner, the patriarch would sit in the corner with his Bible,
and heaven help anybody who disturbed him. Unless his wife
wished to raise some urgent matter relating to his son or two

daughters, the man was to be left alone. After the three children had gone through into the bedroom, his wife would push back the table, and then untie the looped knots that held the mattress in place and roll it out on the floor. This was the signal that it was time for his father to step outside and relieve himself, which allowed his wife the luxury of disrobing in private. However, these days, because the son had left home, and now taken off for England, and because the two daughters had made good marriages to God-fearing local men who seemed unlikely to ever raise a hand to them, Victor imagined that the ritual of the mattress had been discarded and his parents had been able to reclaim the sanctuary of a bedroom for themselves.

The afternoon light was beginning to fade as Peter led the way back to the office. Under Peter's tutelage, Victor's first day as a rent collector had passed by without incident. As they walked, Victor felt a shiver pass through his body, so he turned up the collar of his overcoat against the chill. He looked at Peter, who began to explain that the girl in the office used to live in a room in one of his flats. 'In a house full of women.' Peter gestured dismissively with his arms as he spoke. 'Working girls with painted smiles', he said, and laughed. 'But not my Ruth. Most of my girls are always looking for a gentleman to be kind to them, but I don't accept that sort of payment. Believe me, I have the desire, but during the war I found myself in a place where the doctors were not always your friend.' Again, he laughed. 'But my Ruth is a good girl. She was a student, but I wanted her closer to me, not all the way up there at her college in Harrow.' As Peter talked, Victor looked around. The afternoon streets were busy with both coloured and English people going about their business. Everybody seemed to know Peter, who either touched the brim of his hat, or simply nodded in response to their greetings. 'Do you need a woman, Victor? I can help you with a girl, somebody who you can educate. Or even a woman you might love. You name it, I can help you.'

They walked on, and Victor suspected that it was most probably true that Peter *could* help him to find a girl, but Victor had no intention of wasting his time trying to impress women. Back home he had romanced Lorna under the bridge by the river, and then continued to do so in his room at the back of the piano teacher's house, but now that he was in England the consequences of troubling her weighed heavily upon his mind and he couldn't bring himself to mention Lorna to anybody. Both on the streets, and in the pubs, the swaggering, carefree behaviour of some coloured men towards women unnerved him, for Victor understood that a woman could quickly become an obligation that might keep a man tethered to a mundane life. But today, striding down Golborne Road, with Peter by his side, and suddenly finding himself free of any requirement that he should labour in the cellar of a dreary Notting Hill pub, Victor sensed new possibilities that he had no desire to ruin. He threw a quick glance in Peter's direction, keen to reassure himself that the strange foreign man had not noticed his distaste at the offer to help him with his romantic life, but he need not have worried. Peter was lost in his own thoughts, and he appeared to have now drifted into a reverie that left him oblivious to the good wishes of people on the street. However, at this juncture neither man could possibly have been aware of how life would eventually change for them both. It was a wintry twilight in England, twenty years after the end of the war, and Victor's new employer was wandering back to the office in order that he might collect his attractive young girlfriend and go for cocktails. Victor had been invited to join them. Finally, Victor's prospects in England were looking up.

WHEN PETER FELDMAN FIRST SPOKE to Victor in his thick accent, he told him that he had been led to believe that coloureds might respond better to fellow coloureds knocking on their doors. Furthermore, Peter acknowledged that sending an Englishman to collect rent money meant having to absorb the extra expense of paying for a large Alsatian dog. According to the foreign landlord, coloureds were more likely to pay up if they saw a fierce dog staring at them, but Peter admitted that he was fed up with the inconvenience of feeding a stupid animal. The chubby man had positioned himself on a bar stool in the grimy pub which, at the time, was Victor's place of employment. It was clear that, having never before set foot in the pub, Peter was looking around and trying to assess the situation. The shrewd man had undoubtedly already calculated that if he just gave it a couple of months, there would probably be no need for him to woo Victor, for the coloured man would soon be out of a job. He watched as Peter turned away from the peeling wallpaper and drink-sodden carpet, knocked the ash off the end of his cigar, and then continued to explain things. 'I'm trying hard to give you coloureds a roof over your heads. Somewhere nice and clean to live. You see what I mean, don't you?'

A few days after their conversation in the pub, Victor stepped anxiously into Peter's office, but the squat, balding man was nowhere to be seen. Instead, Victor saw a pretty, long-haired young woman seated behind a desk with a pile of ledgers stacked in front of her. A plate of plain biscuits was balanced precariously on top of the woman's books, and she looked up at Victor but initially said nothing. Once she found her tongue she sat up straight and asked him to take a seat. She offered him tea, which he politely refused. 'So, you're going to start working with us, then? Peter's told me a little bit about you.' Victor watched as she nervously pulled her bright yellow cardigan even tighter around her slim body.

TWO YEARS LATER, Victor paused on the pavement outside a tall house. He still wore his familiar trilby hat and big over-coat, but he now walked with a slight stoop, and he felt heavier—lumpish even. These days, Victor was disenchanted with this line of work, and he approached each morning with a leaden heart. As he looked at the long flight of stairs that led up to the front door, he stamped his feet to keep himself warm. Then he coughed, making sure that his throat was clear, before edging his way down the half-dozen chipped steps which deposited him in front of the basement door. The family were home. The unwelcome cacophony of children screeching at each other split the late afternoon air. It was true that being a rent collector enabled him to get out and about and meet people, and it was far better than working in a pub. Also, because Peter had given him precise instructions, at least he knew exactly what to do, but Victor went about his daily routine without any enthusiasm. He knocked again and this time he heard hushed voices and scurrying feet, and then a bolt was drawn back, and the badly hinged door creaked open a few inches.

'Mr Victor?' The man's face was half-hidden in darkness. 'Maybe you can please wait until tomorrow. I'm sure to have the rent for you by then.'

Victor sighed and bit his bottom lip so he wouldn't immediately say anything he might regret. It didn't give him any pleasure to call upon West Indian tenants and demand rent money, but if they didn't have the means to pay then they shouldn't be in the white man's property. The barefoot immigrant and his wife and their two runny-nosed children appeared as a group in the doorway. Jesus Christ, this fool had no business coming to England and embarrassing himself this way. He didn't blame the woman, for it was the man who should have known better than to bring everybody across the ocean if he didn't have things properly organized. That's what Victor was waiting for, the chance to establish himself before he sent for Lorna and the boy. These things needed to be done with some sober planning. He looked again at the tenant standing in the narrow doorway with his family huddled about him. Had nobody spoken to this man before he set off across the Atlantic Ocean?

'You better give me the money right now or Mr Feldman is going to send somebody to pitch your arse out on the street.'

The door opened a little wider and the man's shiny round face peered out of the gloom, but neither he nor his terrified wife said a word.

'Look, it's the second time I come by here today. It's after five o'clock now and I'm supposed to be somewhere else.'

'Mr Victor, I'm begging you. I can give you a pound now, and I promise that tomorrow I'm going to have the other three pounds.' The forlorn man shooed his wife and children back into the interior of the basement flat and then he lowered his voice to a whisper. 'Mr Victor, if I have to sell my backside in Hyde Park, I'm going to do it, but I'm pleading with you, please don't let Mr Peter put the few things we have out in the damn street. I don't deserve that.'

VICTOR WASN'T TO KNOW it then, but this particular late afternoon encounter marked the beginning of the end of his time working for Peter Feldman. Arguing on doorsteps with fellow West Indians and trying to coerce rent money out of them was, even when things were going smoothly, an unpleasant job. But there was a bigger problem. For the past few months, Victor had been trying to convince himself that he might be able to continue his rent-collecting job while also writing newspaper stories. These days, when he wasn't chasing after Peter's rent money, he could be found in a small, run-down office above a fish-and-chip shop on the Grove where the aloof Claude Westcott edited a two-sheet handout that he proudly called *West Indian News*. Of course, Peter owned the run-down building which housed the newspaper's office, which is how Victor came to meet Claude. Every Wednesday afternoon, he had accustomed himself to the ritual of trudging his way up the stairs and waiting until the

newspaper editor deigned to stop licking his finger and turning the pages of whatever he was reading, and look up from
his desk before disdainfully handing over an envelope that
was always heavy with coins, as if the man was not aware
that English people also offered you the option of money in
the form of paper notes. Victor waited until his second visit
before asking the editor if he might have a copy of *West Indian
News*. Claude looked up, pausing only to make sure that his
superior attitude was firmly in place, and then he informed
Victor that he could have a copy of the newspaper, but only if
Victor gave him threepence in return. The humourless editor
didn't crack a smile, so Victor simply gave him the money
before reaching down and picking up the two folded sheets
that constituted the newspaper.

The following Wednesday, Claude handed over his envelope of rent money and then told Victor that he ought to be
aware that nobody in the community liked what he was doing.
A coloured man exploiting coloured people on behalf of a
white man; did Victor not understand what this kind of thing
looked like? Now it was Victor's turn to assume a superior
attitude. He carefully placed three pennies on the desktop,
picked up the latest edition of *West Indian News*, and left. He
guessed that Claude was maybe around forty, which would
make him only ten years or so older than himself. Who the
hell was this man to talk down to him, telling him what the
West Indian community liked and effectively chastising
him? But despite his immediate suspicion of Claude, Victor
knew that the following week he was going to ask this man if
he might start to write the occasional article for his newspaper,

and when he put his suggestion to the surly editor, he was surprised that the man so readily agreed to let him submit some pieces.

DURING WHAT TURNED OUT TO BE his last few months as a rent collector, Victor would frequently forget the payment schedule for his mind was usually preoccupied with whatever newspaper piece he was currently writing for Claude. On more than one occasion he had knocked at a door and announced, 'I come for the rent money', only to find a tenant staring blankly at him. Victor would stare back at the tenant, but in his head, he would be trying to find the right phrase to describe the dark-skinned girl from Barbados whose mother had, earlier that same morning, stopped him in the street claiming that the girl had just landed a modelling contract in the West End. 'You can write it up, yes?' At the end of the day, an exasperated Peter would often look at Victor and listen as his rent collector blamed the tenants for his own mistakes, and then Peter would smile patiently and try to overlook the mess that Victor had made. 'If the tenants can't pay then you must squeeze them gently, but please, be polite. Everybody deserves some respect, now, don't they, Victor?' In the far corner, and seated behind her desk, Victor could see Ruth, who for some reason would never look directly at him, although he was sure that Mr Feldman's shy secretary-cum-girlfriend understood that the real problem was Victor's lack of commitment to the job of rent-collecting. Once Peter had finished offering up his advice, a winning smile would begin to decorate his pudgy face. In his tuneless voice, Peter would pose his familiar question. 'Shall we three go for a cocktail?'

It was only when Peter went to the bar to get the drinks, that a coy Ruth would raise her eyes from the tabletop, but she always managed to do so without ever turning in Victor's direction. Her discretion—dignity even—was a costume she wore well, and Victor found himself wondering if Peter had helped to dress the young woman in this fashion. He watched as Peter continued to wait impatiently by the bar. His boss always gave out the impression that he was rushing headlong through life; he twitched, and his eyes flitted in every direction, and his unease was palpable. However, despite Victor's dislike of being a rent collector, he couldn't help but feel some affection for this awkward, considerate man whose loneliness looked as though it might at any moment overwhelm him, but who still made the effort to behave as though each day was an occasion for some kind of a party.

ON THE DAY that Victor finally plucked up enough courage to leave Ruth a note declaring that he would like to make a life with her, he wasn't to know that in her mind Ruth had already decided that things could not continue with Peter. They shared a bed, but Peter remained uninterested in her body. It was humiliating. All the more so because she couldn't be certain that, behind her back, Peter wasn't messing about with the tarts in his flats. It was clear that plenty of other blokes fancied her, for she was always getting eyed up in the street. So what was Peter's problem? She had liked it when Paul had finally started to paw her up and down; after all, it was good to be wanted, and her first boyfriend was obviously turned on by her, but Peter's lack of attention caused her to feel both confused and increasingly unhappy. Her first thought on coming back from her lunch break and reading Victor's note was to wonder if she had somehow given off the wrong impression. Victor knew she was Peter's girl, so what made him think he had the right to scribble this kind of a note suggesting that *she* come round to his flat so they could talk about *his* feelings? Nevertheless, it didn't occur to her not to go, for, if nothing else, she needed to give him a piece of her mind. Peter wouldn't be back for the rest of the afternoon, so Ruth picked up her handbag, locked the office door, and marched off to see what Victor had to say for himself. And that's how it began, with not much talking, but both of them understanding that once the door to Victor's grubby little flat was closed shut there could now be no turning back. For the next six weeks, Ruth secretly sneaked around to Victor's flat at every opportunity, but they both knew that things couldn't possibly continue like this.

Eventually, Ruth placed her carefully composed letter on Peter's desk, and set the key to the office on top of it. The previous week, Victor had left Peter to work full-time on *West Indian News*, so Ruth had waited a few days until a distraught Peter appeared to be reluctantly coming to terms with Victor's departure, and only then did she write Peter her brief letter of explanation. She tried to deliver the news sensitively, but she knew there was no way Peter was going to consider her behaviour as anything other than a gross betrayal. Some weeks later, the police showed up at Victor's flat. They let Ruth know that Peter was under investigation for unlawfully evicting tenants, and then they began to ask her all sorts of probing questions. Victor stood to one side and stared defiantly at the officers, while an exasperated Ruth insisted, 'His name is Peter Feldman. Why do you keep asking me what his *real* name is?' It was the same two officers who made the return visits, an older man and a junior one in uniform, and they looked Ruth up and down like she was some kind of a whore, which, given the nature of her living arrangements, is exactly what they thought she was, but Victor never attempted to help out by slipping an arm around her or holding her hand.

CLAUDE HAD AGREED to give Victor a three-month trial as a full-time employee, but after only a fortnight it was clear to the editor that *West Indian News* desperately needed Victor's input if it was going to survive. A second pair of hands would give Claude more time to raise money, which at present came principally from unimaginative advertisements for hairdressers, travel agents, and foodstuff importers. Claude was always struggling to find cash to pay the printers, and when things became difficult, he often had to resort to standing on street corners in the hope of selling additional copies of the newspaper. One morning, Claude took Victor to one side and proposed that they forget the idea of a three-month trial, and Victor 'come on board' permanently. Sensing his indispensability, Victor suggested that Claude might perhaps allow him to sign his articles with the byline 'By Victor Johnson', and although a frustrated Claude was visibly unhappy with the request, he immediately understood that it would serve no purpose to quibble with Victor over this one small point.

Victor's first stories as a permanent employee were commonly reports about dances that had just happened, which the organizers liked to call 'International Dances', for they didn't want to frighten away English people by mentioning the West Indies or the Caribbean. Claude was relieved that he no longer had to attend these tedious Saturday night events, where people on the dance floor often looked like they had fallen asleep while leaning up against each other. Neither music nor dancing appealed to Claude, but with Victor acting as his deputy, Claude was free to spend his time in the pub on a Saturday night, or else he would sit alone in the office and try to work out how he was going to find the money to produce next week's issue. Meanwhile, Victor explained to a disheartened Ruth that going to the international dances was work, therefore he couldn't take her with him. Victor reported on how many people attended these events, and the name of the band, and sometimes he would highlight the individual musicians, and he would often conclude his piece by making some usually ill-informed guess at how much money had been taken at the door. Once in a while, he might suggest to Claude that he be allowed to write a story about a dance that was due to take place, but his editor didn't like to give any space to what was upcoming, for Claude regarded this as free advertising and consequently income lost. Claude and Victor both knew that a Miss West Indies pageant was good material for a big article, as was a walkabout visit from a West Indian politician keen to visit his nationals in England, or the arrival in town of a Negro American celebrity who was due to perform a concert or who was booked for a short stint on the stage of the West End. However, Claude kept these juicier stories for himself. When the West Indies cricket team were playing at Lord's or the Oval, some of the players would habitually wander in the direction of the Grove looking to drink and party with women, and this was always potentially big news, but not news that Claude chose to report, for he would always insist, 'Man, we're not spies.'

Soon enough, the rhythm of Victor's days was quickly established. He would set out in the morning from the claustrophobic flat that he shared with Ruth, and amble the short distance to the newspaper office, always finding a slightly different route to explore. Because he was invariably on the look-out for stories, it could often take him up to an hour, or more, to reach the office on the Grove. Once there, after spending some time conferring with Claude, he would leave and go to a cafe, or the pub, and sit and write up in a notepad whatever thoughts or observations had occurred to him during his morning walk. Why did we never see coloured people delivering milk or pushing letters through people's doors? How many coloured men drove cars in England? Was there a case to be made for sending coloured children to separate schools? Having written up a basic outline for some potential stories, Victor would leave the cafe, or the pub, and return to the office and set the notepad down on his desk and tear out the prospective articles, one to each page, and type them up. Then he would hand them to Claude, who had fallen into the habit of calling Victor his 'street reporter'. Having read them, Claude might have an inconsequential suggestion or two, and Victor generally agreed with his editor, for he knew that the man felt obliged to make some sort of a comment. However, all Victor really cared about was his byline, and the fact that he no longer had to bother with the demeaning nonsense of Peter Feldman's work.

AT SHORTLY AFTER SEVEN TWENTY-FIVE, the bus delivers a weary Ruth to the main gates of the hospital. As the vehicle pulls away from the stop, Ruth wonders if the Polish nurse might be fooled into thinking that Ruth had enjoyed a good night of sleep, but she doubts it. From the moment she first clapped eyes on Danuta, she knew that she was never going to be able to fool this feisty young woman who appears to have taken a shine to her and, while knowing next to nothing about Ruth's past, seems to understand how important it is for Ruth to make an effort to find this man called Peter. Once inside the imposing Victorian brick edifice, Ruth makes her slow way along a corridor whose walls are flecked with a desultory assortment of shadowy spots where the lime-green paint has peeled off. Before Ruth reaches Victor's room she can tell, by the way the West Indian sister is smiling at her from behind her desk at the end of the corridor, that Victor is going to be awake. Ruth says, 'Good morning', and then makes a sharp left and passes through the parted curtains and into Victor's room. She puts her bag down on the plastic chair beside the bed and, as Victor struggles to extend his upturned palm in her direction, carefully drops her hand into his and feels him grasp hold. He tries to smile as he opens his mouth to speak.

'Anybody asking after me?'

There it is, the familiar question. It is more than twenty-five years now since Victor stopped working at the broadsheet newspaper and, ashamed by the manner in which he was let go, practically became a hermit, and to this day he avoids social contact with anybody. Who on earth does he imagine might be asking after him?

'Everything is fine, Victor. Nothing to worry about.'

Of course, Ruth isn't going to tell Victor about Lucy's visit, for that would only antagonize him. Despite his circumstances, Victor still clings determinedly to a fierce sense of pride, and Ruth continues to do her best to protect him. However, over the years, Victor has not aged gracefully, and his grey hair is now manifestly thinning, and his stoop has become even more pronounced. Once his severance money ran out, Victor was able to claim unemployment benefit, but this eventually stopped when he began to receive his state pension. Victor's lack of money has been yet another source of shame for him, so Ruth always tries to steer clear of this subject, and any other issues that might rile Victor. Naturally, her daughter comes under the heading of topics that might rub Victor up the wrong way.

Ruth first noticed Victor's increasing defensiveness when he stopped working with Claude and started to write for the national newspaper. It was then that Victor's nature became difficult to endure, for, in addition to his secretiveness, he also became tetchy. He gradually stopped asking for Ruth's help with the research for his articles, and so her trips to the borough library petered out. She wanted to ask Victor what he imagined her role in his life might be, now that he appeared to have outgrown her professionally, but she deemed it best to say nothing and simply wait until Victor seemed ready to share with her once again. Sadly, she soon began to come to terms with the fact that this was unlikely to happen. Having moved beyond Claude, she could see that Victor was now out of his depth in this new job, but he steadfastly refused to discuss his feelings with her. Victor's contributions to the national newspaper were hardly stories; they could more properly be described as superficial reports culled from agency information or local government printouts. During the street riots in the early eighties, things improved a little as Victor was dispatched to report on the violence in both Bristol and Liverpool. However, once things calmed down it was clear to Ruth that his bosses seemed unsure what to do with him. As she struggled to accommodate the unhappiness that Victor's new job was visiting on both of their lives, Ruth cast her mind back and realized that the always perceptive Peter had noticed Victor's insecurity long before anybody else. Ruth had often witnessed Peter sliding a protective arm around Victor's shoulders and assuring him, 'We're brothers, Victor. English orphans. In this country we have to work hard and make it on our own.' But when she thought about it, Ruth realized that she never once heard Victor respond to the conciliatory words of his eager-sounding 'brother'.

Ruth stares at Victor in his hospital bed and tries to banish Peter from her thoughts. She can sense the physical pain that Victor is trying hard to disguise, then, releasing her hand from his, she reaches into her bag for a handkerchief which she uses to carefully dab Victor's perspiring forehead. Lucy was right; he had lied to her, but didn't everybody have things that they wished to hide and hoped might never surface into the judgmental light of day? Once the truth about Lorna began to emerge, Ruth swallowed her pride and tried to explain to a chastened Victor that people often behaved in ways that they knew would necessitate lying to themselves, and to others, but she wanted him to understand that she could move past this deception. But what choice did she have? She had effectively isolated herself from her family, and she had no friends, so accepting the humiliation, and waiting for Victor to come back to her, seemed like her only option. It was only later, when she got the letter from Lucy's social worker, that the possibility of another kind of life began to appear on the horizon. However, her daughter's stubborn refusal to accommodate Victor means that this idea of a new life remains little more than a remote possibility. As Ruth lowers her eyes to look again at Victor, she can see that the grey-haired man is now drifting back to sleep.

Ruth remembers that after Victor deserted Peter for full-time work at *West Indian News*, the orphans would every so often run into each other on the street. One afternoon, Ruth happened to be by Victor's side, as he was making his way to Claude's office, when they saw Peter. Ruth could discern that Peter no longer felt so brotherly, and his rheumy-eyed smile couldn't disguise the fact that he remained dumbfounded by the double betrayal. When Peter first realized that Victor had defected, he quickly offered to make Victor a partner in his ailing company, a gesture which struck Ruth as typically generous but foolish. Surely Peter was not so desperate for a friend? He was a businessman who, as far as she was able to make out, never allowed his emotions to cloud his judgment. Of course, by the time Victor moved on from *West Indian News*, in his attempt to become somebody on Fleet Street, Peter had long since disappeared, and Ruth imagined that

Victor had effectively forgotten him. After all, Victor had other things on his mind. He was now beginning to receive the occasional invitation to be interviewed on television and on the radio, and with his newly minted broadsheet credentials he was keen to be regarded as *the* journalist who recorded and explained the activities of coloured people in Mrs Thatcher's Britain. Ruth watched as Victor tried to grow into this more visible role, but it was disturbingly clear to her, and presumably to his new employers, that Victor really didn't know how to play the part. There were many dinners or receptions at which Victor would drink too much, and then say something which would irritate a guest, and Ruth always knew that this was her cue to quickly usher Victor out of the venue. Ruth understood that some people felt obliged to invite Victor to such events, despite the fact that his presence often made them uncomfortable, but she knew that it wasn't her place to try to persuade headstrong Victor to stay away from such gatherings, even though they made him unhappy.

The one time Ruth tried to carefully explain what *she* was seeing, an angry Victor gave her the silent treatment and slowly, and perhaps inevitably, their relationship began to fall into even greater disrepair. When the newspaper eventually let Victor go ('I'm afraid we're presently overstaffed'), Ruth watched as he accepted the redundancy package with sullen resignation. Ruth tried to maintain Victor's spirits as he spoke, without enthusiasm, about writing a book about black soldiers who had taken part in the Falklands War, but she knew there would be no book. Victor's drinking was out of control, and it was around this time that Lorna began to telephone Ruth on a daily basis and rant, while at other times

Lorna simply droned on in a monotone until Ruth could take no more and she would end the call by firmly replacing the receiver. Ruth never passed on any of Lorna's barbed messages to Victor, nor did she speak to him about the insults directed at herself, for it was apparent that Victor had enough demons to contend with. He certainly didn't need to be reminded of Lorna's state of mind, nor his estrangement from his wayward son.

It is early afternoon when Ruth opens her heavy eyes and looks down at Victor, whose breathing remains deep and regular. She glances around and can see the West Indian sister standing in the doorway watching her. The bulky woman takes a step forward and whispers that the doctor would like to speak with her. The sister insists that Ruth should go along to the doctor's office as soon as possible and, as if to underscore the urgency of the situation, she glances at her wristwatch as she speaks. However, before Ruth has a chance to ask why it is so important that she presents herself for an audience with the doctor, the sister turns and begins to gingerly walk away on her heavily cushioned soles. Ruth looks again at Victor, who, unperturbed by the sudden tension in the atmosphere, continues to sleep. Unsure of what else to do, an anxious Ruth rises slowly to her feet, tucks some loose strands of hair behind both ears, reclaims her bag, and moves off in the direction of the doctor's office.

RUTH'S MOTHER, Beryl, had been determined to raise her only child so that she grew up to be a polite young woman. She liked to point out to her husband that just because she was a shopkeeper's wife in a dreary south Yorkshire town didn't mean that she wasn't allowed to harbour ambitions for her daughter. She introduced Ruth to ballet classes, but when it became clear that *pas de deux* meant little to her child she insisted on taking her to ballroom dancing lessons, where Ruth pirouetted with one graceless boy after another, although her mother insisted that conversations with the opposite sex were to be avoided at all costs. In fact, her mother was careful to make sure her daughter never partnered the same boy on successive Saturdays. When, against all the odds, Ruth passed the eleven-plus examination, it transpired that the five schools that her mother had listed as options were all single-sex institutions, with the two Catholic schools being her mother's preferred choices even though the family had no religious affiliations.

St Theresa's Girl's High boasted a strict dress code, with inflexible regulations about the length of girls' skirts and detailed instructions as to how the pupils were expected to wear their hair. Across the wide expanse of the playing fields was St Thomas's Boys School. By the fifth form, despite her own flat-fronted condition, Ruth had somehow been admitted into a small circle of popular girls with well-developed busts. The girls soon contrived a way to meet the more interesting St Thomas's boys behind the school pavilion for cigarettes, although, as the year progressed, she soon twigged that some girls were meeting up for more than just a smoke. But not Ruth, at least not to begin with, for although she was interested in going a little further than occasionally locking eyes with a boy, she was helplessly shy. Then, shortly after the Easter holidays, Ruth fell into conversation with a sixth-former,

Paul Hirst, who held his cigarettes like a film star and combed his hair like Cliff Richard, and everything began to change. Ruth untied her ponytail, the hem of her skirt crept up an inch or two, and predictably her grades plummeted. Conversations with her mother became more intense, and then collapsed into shouting matches as Beryl reminded her daughter that when her father came back from Malaya or Burma, or wherever he claimed to be, and put her with child, it was her mother who had to give up her job in the steelworks, and miss VE Day celebrations, and then struggle to feed three mouths while rationing was still in full swing, while her father just went back behind the counter like nothing had happened. What's more, Beryl let her know that, although it was many years ago now, she had still to get over the fact that during the war she had lost her own mum and dad to a bomb that had reduced her parents' home in Sheffield to a pile of rubble. There was little point in Ruth turning to her father for support, for she had never managed to develop much of a relationship with the tightly wound man, who tried hard to hide his volatile temper as he diligently catered to the customers in his hardware shop. In the evenings, much to Beryl's dismay, Ruth's father would occupy himself with the daily task of balancing the books and seeing to his accounts. That's when the arguments would begin, and her parents made precious little effort to disguise the antipathy they obviously felt for each other.

When Paul Hirst entered her life, with his tight trousers and pencil-thin tie, Ruth quickly recognized that he was more level-headed than the other boys. She tried to make it clear to him that she was up for taking a chance should he choose to reach for the buttons on her blouse, but as far as she could tell her suitor appeared to be content to draw the line at holding hands or giving her the odd side hug. Ruth tried to put him on the spot by *accidentally* letting him see a bit of bra strap, but she soon stopped her games as she had no desire to come across as a common bit of goods. Walks with Paul along the riverbank, during which time he flaunted his knowledge of fishing and shared his dream of one day owning a canal barge, seemed glamorous; as did coffee with him, in the new pseudo-Italian espresso bar in the town centre, where egg and chips, bread and butter, and Tizer were not to be found anywhere on the menu, although the brightly coloured plastic tablecloths that were tacked under at the corners suggested that these items might one day reappear should the fad for frothy coffee run its course. Paul often talked about maybe joining the French Foreign Legion, and he opened Ruth's mind to a different world, but having listened intently for weeks on end, Ruth soon had to admit that it was not a world that truly excited her. Just when she was beginning to wonder whether she should chuck this boyfriend, a newly animated Paul seemed to have decided that it was now time to take things to the next stage, and with the cold precision of a military campaign, he made it his business to breach Ruth's outer garments and press on into her undergarments, and before long she discovered herself pregnant.

On the fateful April afternoon that they sat together on a park bench, and Ruth broke the news to Paul, she saw his face begin to immediately flush. Paul swallowed deeply, then insisted that he wasn't ready to become a father or get married. Ruth turned her head slightly so that this boy wouldn't be able to see that she was so angry she had started to cry. She hadn't asked Paul Hirst to marry her. Who the bloody hell did he think he was? Later that evening, Paul's irate mother and father visited her parents' flat above the hardware shop, and all four adults crammed into the small living room for a conversation that seemed to go on for an age. When Paul's folks finally left, Ruth was summoned into the presence of her parents and her grim-faced mother informed her that a decision had been made. Ruth opened her mouth to speak, but Beryl pushed a finger into her daughter's face. 'I didn't bring you up to be a slag, and I went out of my way to make sure that you didn't go to a pram-pusher school. I did everything for you, and this is how you repay me?'

Seven months later, a tall, tweed-suited man and his equally smartly attired wife showed up at the local hospital and hovered awkwardly by the door to Ruth's room. Before Ruth had properly learned how to hold her daughter, a nurse approached and carefully removed the soft bundle from her arms. The nurse carried the child from the room and out into the corridor where, through the large glass window in the door, Ruth was able to see her daughter's new mother and father taking delivery of *their* child. After Ruth left hospital, Beryl decided that having taken nearly a whole academic year off from school, her daughter should now go back to St Theresa's. In fact, she screamed and insisted that Ruth do so, and as she spat out her frustration, a cold shiver passed through her daughter and carried away any residual affection she may have had for Beryl. At school, Ruth ignored the judgmental stares of the other girls, and decided instead to pour her energies into her schoolwork. It was a concerned

Miss Simpson, her sympathetic form mistress, who eventually suggested that Ruth might want to consider applying to take a secretarial course in Harrow, which was near London. At the end of one school day, she asked Ruth to stay behind and informed her that, having sent the institution a letter of enquiry, she had now heard that the college could offer Ruth a place, and they also provided accommodation for their girls. Miss Simpson intimated that it would do Ruth some good to put a little distance between herself and bad memories, although they both understood that in reality Miss Simpson was trying to help Ruth break free of her mother.

Miss Simpson took it upon herself to speak privately with Ruth's father, who, recognizing the fractured relationship between his overbearing wife and his teenage daughter, decided that the schoolteacher's proposed course of action made sense. He shook Miss Simpson's hand and promised her that, having assiduously put aside a few bob each week out of the wage packet that he paid himself, he would dip into his savings and find the necessary fees to send his daughter on this 'commercial course'. And so it came to pass. Soon after enrolling at the college, eighteen-year-old Ruth met a distinctly overweight Peter Feldman, with his flash car and spiffy smile, when the foreigner swaggered into the building looking for secretarial help for his purported organization. It had been explained to Ruth that prospective employers might occasionally turn up at the college offering work experience, and although Ruth understood that she was not yet in any way qualified, her hazel eyes lit up, for she knew that getting a paying job, however modest, might mean never again having to go home and live under the same roof as her mother.

Later, she would tell Victor that Peter had *rescued* her, and she owed him for that. But when Victor first came into Peter's basement office, she studiously avoided saying much of anything to the coloured fellow in the trilby hat. Beneath his overcoat, the man wore a fashionable jacket with skinny lapels, and he had a loose-limbed, moderately stooped body. His face was open, kind even, but Ruth was mindful not to make any eye contact. On that first day, as they both waited for Peter to return to the office, Ruth sipped at her tea, and pulled her canary yellow cardigan even tighter around her shoulders, before picking up a biscuit from the plate that was carefully balanced on top of the ledgers on her desk.

THE DOCTOR ASKS RUTH to close the door behind her. She does as he requests and then sits down heavily on the chair in front of his desk. For some reason, the chair is set at a slightly quirky angle, and so she stands up, straightens the chair, and then sits back down again. Ruth looks closely at the doctor and swallows deeply. She thinks, 'I've been with Victor for a long time, so you had better tell me the truth.' But the doctor keeps scanning the papers on his desk and won't meet her gaze. She thinks again of Peter, and how she treated him, and wonders if the Polish nurse has any more news for her. Once she has finished here, she will go to find Danuta and ask her. Meanwhile, is this man ever going to bloody well look up? On top of his desk, Ruth can see a nicely framed photograph of his wife and two children. She has never seen a picture of Victor before England. She has also never seen a picture of Victor's parents. She wonders; does he look like them? Does he resemble his father? Her heart sinks a little, for she realizes that she experienced some of the same humiliating confusion about Peter's past, although Peter had once allowed her a brief glimpse of a small photograph of his parents, and there had also been a framed picture of Peter's mother beside their bed. Perhaps Lucy is right; does she truly know who Victor is? Mind you, Victor has never seen a picture of *her* parents, but this is more explicable, for, not long after she moved to London, she tried to stop thinking about them, and she has no photograph of either parent, let alone one of them together. They finally divorced when her father eventually caught on to what had been going on between his best mate, Len, and his wife. It was then that her father made the decision to go off to Spain and live with his brother and apply himself to some gardening. After her mother's death, her father wrote and spilled the whole truth about Beryl's many infidelities over the years, and then he told her about the sadness that cast a shadow over his ex-wife's final months. Beryl and Len had tried to make a go of it running an antiques shop in the Peak District, and then her mother was struck down with cancer—the type which moves rapidly and without compassion—and that was it. A year after her mother's death, Princess Diana was killed in Paris. Her father wrote Ruth another long, but to her mind heartless, letter informing her that he wouldn't be coming back to 'sad' England. Even though he had a daughter, he claimed that he didn't see any point in returning, as the country now appeared to be run by foreigners, and so he'd be stopping on the Costa.

Ruth stares at the top of the doctor's bald head and once

again torments herself with the problem of what to do about Victor. Was she stupid to have stuck by Victor once he told her about Lorna and the child? Clearly that's what her daughter thinks, and Lucy has been urging her to leave him the way she left Peter. And then do what? Who the hell is going to have a hankering to take on a relic like her? Ruth hears the doctor telling her that Victor can go home this weekend. She can take him home? Ruth continues to stare at the smiling doctor and wonders if this is a joke. The doctor speaks, while offering her the kind of sympathetic look that fills Ruth with hostility, but she doesn't hear any more of the man's words. She can take Victor home? The hospital is finished with him? Just like that? Ruth hears the commotion of the doctor's chair scraping against the hard plastic floor as he stands up, and then the balding man extends his hand across the desk in a gesture of farewell while still wearing his stupid smile.

Ruth sits on the chair to the side of Victor's bed and, in a quiet whisper, tells the willowy Polish nurse what the doctor has said. Danuta wears her hair in a single auburn plait that has fallen out of her cap, and so today she has draped it casually over her right shoulder and tucked the end into her collar. The nurse listens and nods her head, but she appears to be untroubled by the doctor's words. Instead, she changes the subject and tells Ruth that she is 'sorry'. She asked at the Polish Club, and she even went to the Old People's Centre, where most of the elderly congregate, but nobody had heard of this 'Peter'. Ruth knows that a part of her never really believed that Danuta would be able to solve the riddle of Peter's disappearance, but she is grateful to her for trying. Danuta continues. 'One man, a retired university professor, he offered to go to the library to help.' Danuta shrugs. 'He has the time. Is this something you would wish for?' Ruth takes young Danuta's hands in her own and bounces them gently to reassure her.

'No, thank you. You've done all you can. Really, thank you.'

Danuta shrugs her shoulders. 'I will tell the old man. But, if you change your mind, you must promise to let me know. I think he is genuine in his desire to help.'

Ruth watches as Danuta turns and leaves her alone with a sleeping Victor. She knows that she should have asked the nurse if the doctor was really trying to tell her that they've given up on Victor. Is this what's going on? If so, the doctor needs to be straight with her and stop treating her like a child. He's one of those self-assured arses she longs to see stumble over a crack in the pavement and fall flat on his face. But she understands that nothing ever seems to trip up men like him.

SHORTLY AFTER STARTING WORK for Peter, Ruth discovered that travelling back and forth from Harrow to Notting Hill was something of a chore. Her new boss agreed and arranged to move her into a rented room in one of his flats and then later, as the nature of their relationship changed, into a house which the two of them would share. Peter Feldman was something of an enigma. It was a word, like many others, that he taught his young companion. He instinctively licked his dry thin lips before smiling, and then he would declare,

'My love, I'm going to teach you everything I know.' However, after nearly a year in which Ruth tried hard to convince herself that she was reasonably happy, Peter suddenly stopped bothering to point out new words to her. She wanted to ask him why, but to do so would have been to open the door to another one of his lectures that she was beginning to suspect were designed for the sole purpose of making her feel as 'daft as a brush'—this being a phrase her father often used when referring to customers who annoyed him. Ruth told Peter this, and other somewhat uncomfortable things about her upbringing, hoping that she might break through his reserve and get him to talk about the mystery that was Peter Feldman, but nothing ever seemed to succeed. She knew that there must have been a life before England, but whenever she warily quizzed him about this, Peter offered her a brief nod of his head and then he niftily changed tack. He was prepared to talk about the dingy hostel he lived in once he arrived in England, and the kind of work he did which eventually led to his becoming a landlord, but he kept the door shut on anything that might have taken place before London. He was never abrupt or offhand, for this was not Peter's style; he simply swerved, and Ruth would suddenly realize that they were now talking about something completely different and so, although Peter clearly didn't approve, she may as well go back to reading her copy of *Honey* magazine or watching *Ready Steady Go!* on the television set.

OCCASIONALLY, PETER CAUGHT SIGHT of a bemused Ruth staring at the photograph of his mother that he kept on the table to the side of the bed. The studio photographer had captured a beautiful woman in a sealskin coat, whose blond hair was drawn back and held together in a bun on the back of her head. Her high forehead was a feature that his mother was unashamedly proud of, and around her neck she wore a discreet gold necklace that Peter's besotted father had given her, along with the many other gifts that he couldn't afford. The family lived modestly in a three-room apartment, but even this frugal lifestyle was beyond the means of a tailor whose business in a respectable, but by no means fashionable, part of the town centre merely limped along from one week to the next. At home the family didn't have the means to engage a housekeeper or a cook, but at his place of work his father employed Simon, an elderly assistant-cum-part-time-cleaner to help keep the oftentimes unkempt premises in order. However, his embarrassed mother had long ago stopped bringing their only child to the ramshackle shop to meet his father at the end of the day. Maria tried to introduce Peter to music lessons, but from the moment young Peter sat clumsily on his first piano stool his lack of musical talent became painfully evident. She bristled when the ancient music teacher described her son as 'a well-fed boy with a cabbage head who should never be allowed near an instrument', and she refused to pay the woman. Dance classes proved equally disastrous, and her son's reluctance to partner with the girls stirred a far greater anxiety than any that might be occasioned by his failure to master even the simplest of steps.

As they left the dance studio, for what his mother had determined would be the final time, she took Peter's hand. 'Because you've been a good boy, perhaps we should call in at

Leo's and buy some sweets.' Peter looked up and shook off
her playful hair tousle, but he said nothing, for he suspected
that his overwrought mother would immediately forget any
plans to visit Leo's. As they walked together, he despaired,
for it upset him that his feet seemed incapable of following
instructions. Peter was eager to please the beautiful woman
wearing a vivid red scarf, whose deep frustration with life he
had already detected at an age when children should be spared
the indignity of seeing weakness in their parents. He had already surmised that the family's three-room apartment was
most likely rudimentary compared to other boys' homes, and
he could sense his mother's unhappiness with their lowly status. Their apartment was an attic walk-up, the cheapest in
the building, and therefore lacking even the most basic facil-
ities, although they were spared the inconvenience of having
to fetch water from a well. However, every time they wished
to relieve themselves his family had to submit to the shame
of a tedious journey down three flights of stairs to the court-
yard toilet at the back of the building. The neighbours were a
mixed lot, and the pungent smell of cooking often filled the
communal staircase, as did the noises of shouting and door-
slamming that disturbed the peace at all hours. These days,
the steep trudge to the top floor was becoming burdensome
for both of Peter's parents although, despite his being a visibly
heavyset boy, the numerous stairs hardly troubled him. As
Peter and his mother continued to walk away from Leo's,
Peter thought of the colourful sweets on the counter in large
glass jars, beneath which were hidden trays which held choc-
olates wrapped in gold foil, neatly arranged in rows like obe-
dient soldiers. These treats would only become detectable

when the drawers were ceremoniously pulled out but, as he had suspected, the promise of sweets from Leo's had entered and then left his poor mother's head in an instant.

His father doted on his only child. No matter how long Peter's hapless extracurricular activities might last, he always arrived back from school before his father, who he would hear dragging himself up the stairs. Once inside, the tired man would customarily slump into a chair in the corner of the room and look wistfully at his wife and son, who would be seated at the wooden table having already finished supper. 'How was your day?' It was never entirely clear who the exhausted man was addressing—wife or son—but because these days his mother seldom responded, Peter felt a responsibility to spare his weary father the discomfort of silence.

'Everything is fine, Papa.'

Eventually his father would stand and take a step in the direction of his son, and then run his hand through the black hair that resembled his own, before taking a seat at the table and waiting for his wife to place a plate before him.

'Good, Peter. Pay attention to your schoolwork. Your way out of here is your books.' This was how Peter remembered his parents. His determined father, and his poor mother, who was unable to disguise her disappointment with the match her own father had secured for her. The promise of the young tailor, with a talent for both making and mending clothes, had long ago faded. The ambition that Maria's father had encouraged her to anticipate had failed to materialize. It was clear to Peter that his father was a perfectionist and an honest man, but his father didn't seem to be able to recognize that his wife would stoop to almost anything in order that she might appear before the world as a success. The man's mind was preoccupied with his business. Single- or double-breasted? Padded shoulders or tapered at the waist? Double pleats? Cuffs to the trousers? These days, rather than consider Maria's needs, he would grapple with the question of whether he needed to restock the ribbons and the buttons and the laces that he sold, or first order more fabric that the customers might buy to fashion garments for themselves.

After dinner, Peter would watch his mother standing by the sink, knowing that her greatest wish was that the hopes once invested in her husband might now be realized in her son. As far as Peter could see, she continued to do her duty, making his father's food, sharing his bed, attending to him whenever he caught a cold or a chill, but it was clear to Peter that she had long ceased to expect anything in return. Meanwhile, his mother's hopes for her son were becoming increasingly desperate, and Peter would catch her stealing glances at him as though wondering what she might be able to do to usher him along a path to a successful life. However, as the world about them became increasingly bleak, Peter sensed that such worries would soon become irrelevant, for the ability to control the direction of their own lives was already slipping from their grasp.

THREE YEARS LATER, Peter was now beginning to think of himself as a young man, as opposed to a boy, but he still had little idea how he might help his parents. His mother's erratic behaviour had continued to escalate, and in the mornings he would lie in bed and listen as she stumbled about in the kitchen and held conversations with herself. His mother made no effort to keep down the noise, and it was clear that she was trying to draw attention to herself. Clearly, Maria wanted to talk, but Peter feared the confessional intimacy that she desired. The music lessons and dance classes were far behind them, but Peter had not, like other boys, replaced these pastimes with an interest in sport, or the pursuit of girls, nor had he developed any illicit habits such as the smoking of cigarettes or drinking. Peter had nothing to offer his mother that might mollify her turmoil, and nothing to hide from her, beyond a growing conviction that it might be best for everyone if he left both the apartment and their town and went in search of some other place where he might begin anew and thus release his mother from her anxieties about his future. Peter had no desire to share these thoughts with his mother, and so he lay in bed with his eyes closed and listened to the agitated woman rattling about in the kitchen. As the darkness of night slowly gave way to dawn, the sounds of confusion grew louder, but Peter had little understanding of how he might usefully offer his mother the comfort of his support.

At school, Peter often caught himself gazing out the window at the trams in the street below, or staring at the birds roosting on the windowsill of the tall office building across the street that blocked the light from his classroom. For the greater part of the day, Peter's mind would remain studiously adrift from the teacher and his fellow pupils. Sometimes he would torment himself with the idea that he should go to visit his father's tailor's shop and make sure that his father was all right. He would try to imagine how he might build a secret relationship with this tranquil man, but what would father and son say to each other? Whenever Peter gathered up his books at the end of the day, and then passed out onto the street, his resolve would fail him, for he knew that his father would be busy, and should he turn up unannounced the poor man would be unsure what to do with his son. As a result, Peter would slowly amble his way back to the three-room apartment, where he would usually discover his mother sitting alone in the kitchen. She would look up at him, but the dejected woman could barely bring herself to ask her child about his day. The truth was mother, father, and son were slowly drifting apart.

'Good afternoon, Mama.'

His mother smiled, but in doing so she simply revealed her age. Formerly, her appearance had meant everything to Maria, and her dignity depended upon the early rooting-out of a grey hair, or the assiduous plucking of a too-bushy eyebrow. These days, the face that his mother wore wasn't her own. She would get up from the table and move over to the stove and light a flame under the kettle. Her son would sit down and begin the rigmarole of emptying his bag of schoolbooks and stacking them before himself. Why, he wondered, did he never go to his father and tell him of his misgivings; talk to him about his concern for his mother, and his uncertainty about the future? Was this the end of his childhood? If so, how had he managed to undertake this journey to the threshold of adulthood without accumulating any real friends? Peter stared at his books. Perhaps his father was right. Perhaps his books were his way out of this situation. But what did his father really know? Perhaps he was merely acting the role of father. To Peter, everything seemed to be a performance. Peter determined this was what he truly felt about life. It all appeared to be some kind of theatre, and Peter was simply trying to speak his lines to the best of his abilities. What more could anybody want from him?

IT WAS AN UNUSUALLY COLD SPRING MORNING when Peter's mother, her hand clasped firmly around her son's arm, ushered him in the direction of the train station. They walked together in silence, their faces stinging in the biting wind, carefully sidestepping the evidence of another night of broken windows. Soon there would be war; everybody knew this. The only questions were, when would the conflict truly begin and how long would it last? In the meantime, despite Peter's objections, his mother had insisted that he should be sent to a safer location. She had explained her reasons to him with a purse-lipped brevity, and Peter listened in bewildered silence and tried to imagine what life might be like on his aunt and uncle's farm. They had visited his mother's sister just once, when he was perhaps five years old, but he had no real memories of the place beyond the barking dogs in the yard and the awful smell of the animals. Peter had no desire to return, and his father clearly shared his feelings of disquiet. For the past week, he had listened to his parents arguing in the evening once they thought Peter might be asleep. His frustrated father tried repeatedly to convince his mother that there was little need for alarm, for his tailoring business offered the townspeople a useful service and customers still treated his family with respect. After all, they were not religious people, and they did not go out of their way to advertise their origins or their beliefs. Both at home and at work, they spoke the national language. However, his mother's ferocity could not be assuaged, and she laughed at the idea that needles and threads might save them. Maria insisted that even if her husband was correct and they continued to be spared harassment, when war broke out their son was likely to be pressed into serving in the army. Is this what he wanted for their only child? Once this point had been shrilly made, there was usually nothing further that passed between husband and wife, and Peter was finally able to tug the blanket to his chin and attempt to find some sleep.

Mother and son slowly approached the ominous, soot-blackened palace that was the train station. The building sat up high like an ornate black cathedral, and it dwarfed all constructions in every direction. As they entered the station, Peter could see that his mother was fighting back tears. She avoided looking in his direction, for clearly the confluence of emotions was too knotted and, as far as he could guess, his mother was most likely feeling both shame and despair in equal measure. Shame that she was sending him away at a time when most parents were clinging ever closer to their children, and despair that she might not be able to save her son. Whenever his parents quarrelled, Peter could always hear his father's increasingly indignant voice insisting that his wife's childless older sister, and her dolt of a husband, had little experience of life beyond their own small country circle. How could these peasants possibly know how to address the issues of a town boy like Peter, who was standing on the edge of manhood? Allegedly, his aunt had, at her marriage, renounced her background and taken up the traditions of the majority. Consequently, Peter's mother hoped that her son might temporarily disappear into her sister's world until this storm passed. His mother hissed that she was not sending her son away, she was simply encouraging him to hide until they could once again be together. Or would her husband prefer that she do nothing, and the family just wait for the knock on the door? As mother and son pushed their way onto a crowded platform, Peter watched as she handed him a train ticket. Then she pulled a letter to her sister from her bag and thrust it in her son's direction.

'Do you have the food?' As soon as his mother asked the question, she must have realized how stupid she sounded, for the neat packet that she had prepared was already tucked under his arm. An apple, a hunk of bread, and some cheese would have to suffice for the three-hour journey. Across Peter's back was slung a rucksack into which his mother had instructed him to stuff some clothes, and whatever books he wished to take.

'You must write and let us know that you have arrived safely, and perhaps from time to time you might tell us how you are.'

But Peter could see the worry on his mother's face. After all, she had warned him that his aunt might quiz him as to whether he had brought money for his food and lodging, and make him feel as though he was a burden that was being foisted upon her. His mother had been unsparing in her condemnation of her sister, making it clear that once his aunt had accepted the marriage proposal from her tall, unprepossessing farmer, the woman had never given much thought to anybody but herself.

After a perfunctory kiss on the cheek from her son, Maria watched Peter mount the three steps to the train and then disappear inside, only to reappear a few moments later as he took a seat by the window. He peered down at her through the glass, and then an earsplitting whistle sounded, and she listened to the coughing and groaning as the steam train began to noisily belch its way out of the station. Maria raised an ungloved hand, and her son did the same, but unlike the other passengers, Peter chose not to open the window and he soon vanished behind a thick veil of smoke. Maria waited until the clamour had faded, and the train had passed safely into the distance, before turning and walking in the direction of the station's grand hall, and then back out onto the street, where it had now begun to rain.

As she entered the cafe, Maria saw a table in the far corner by the huge window, upon which was stencilled in gold lettering the name of the establishment. She sat heavily in one of the two chairs and waited for the waiter to approach with his pad and pen. She ordered coffee and a pastry, and then decided that when she left the cafe she would go to her husband's tailor shop and surprise him. It was just the two of them now, and perhaps Peter's departure would allow them the opportunity to rebuild a relationship with each other, an idea which, much to her surprise, vaguely appealed to her. Perhaps she would give her husband another chance to prove himself, and this time she would try not to be so hasty in her judgment. As her thoughts meandered, Maria noticed a man, across the other side of the cafe, whose silver hair fell louchely over his collar. This bohemian touch aside, everything about the dapper yet fastidious man suggested that he was a success in the world. She lowered her eyes, and looked up again, and now she was sure; there could be no doubt that the man was gazing in her direction. The elderly waiter brought her order to the table, and she thanked him. As he moved away, she took the opportunity to glance at the window, where she could see the reflection of the silver-haired man, whose casual inspection had now hardened into a hostile stare that lacked any suggestion of kindness. Because of this unpleasantness, she now understood that it might be wise to abandon her coffee and pastry. She quickly gathered up her things and hurried out into the cold morning drizzle and, having decided not to visit her husband at his place of work, quickly set off in the direction of the empty apartment.

That evening, Maria sat together with her husband at the kitchen table. The two of them toyed with their bowls of soup and for the first time in many years, given the absence of Peter, she felt truly alone. Her husband looked up and asked if everything was all right. All right? She wanted to scream but chose instead to continue to silently spoon the soup into her mouth. Her husband was a mystifyingly timid man. That much was clear for all to see, but she periodically wondered if she was perhaps responsible for killing something inside him. Is this what had happened to her husband? Had some part of him tried and failed to please her, and thereafter shrivelled in defeat? Had she damaged him? Later, Maria found herself standing at the sink, while her placid

husband sat in his chair and read the newspaper. She surrep-
titiously pulled a handkerchief from her apron and wiped her
eyes. Tomorrow she would fashion her blond hair into a tidy
bun and decorate her cheeks with a smear of pink blush.
She would wear her most treasured possession, her red scarf.
The man in the cafe with the silver hair. Would he be there
tomorrow? Perhaps she had misread the hardening of this
man's gaze.

PETER PRESSED HIS FACE to the window of the carriage and
watched as the town eventually disappeared and the land-
scape became dominated by grass, animals, and then small
clusters of houses that gathered together to form villages. He
realized that the filth on the windows, that were now streaked
with thin rivers of rain, was simply debris from earlier jour-
neys. The train dawdled, and for no ostensible reason made
frequent, and seemingly irrational, stops, sometimes in the
middle of fields. He could hear clanging and shouting outside, but nobody got on or off and then, just as suddenly and
mysteriously as the train had ground to a halt, it would start
up again and move off on its slow way. Two nuns shared his
compartment, and although the younger of the women
seemed keen to engage him in polite conversation, the older
one was stern-faced and clearly determined to maintain some
distance from the strange-looking young man who appeared
as though he might well be running away from something.
Their neglect meant that, before arriving at his destination,
Peter had time to turn over in his mind once again the hurtful

dilemma that his fiercely resolute mother had decided to send him away, and that his father had made no real effort to intervene on his behalf.

The farm was smaller than he remembered. In fact, it was little more than three fields, one of which held cows, one sheep, and the third, and biggest, was planted with crops, which he guessed were principally potatoes and wheat. In this third field stood a small barn, an outhouse, and a flimsy shelter beneath which bales of hay were stored. At supper on the first evening, his tall uncle sat at the kitchen table, with its ill-fitting embroidered linen cloth, and scratched his bearded face. He began to boast of his plans for expansion, but he chewed and spoke at the same time, exposing his food and spitting the occasional speck in his nephew's direction. Peter listened, but his attention was drawn to the mobile hands of the so-called landowner, for his uncle's wedding ring was sunk uncomfortably deep into the meat of his finger, and the man's knuckles were swollen with arthritis. His grim-faced aunt lingered by the squat-legged stove and, although she intermittently lifted a bowl of milk to her mouth, she chose to say nothing.

Later, Peter lay in bed and stared through the uncovered window at a sky that was speckled with stars. There were no streetlamps, and no houses with brightly lit windows, and the overwhelming, ominous quiet disturbed him. Peter recalled that the previous week his father had asked him to visit his tailor shop after school, but he insisted that Peter not mention anything to his mother. Father and son sat together in the back room, away from the prying eyes of customers and the ears of his father's assistant, and, as his father spoke, Peter learned about his relatively prosperous maternal grandparents, and how disillusioned they had been with the marriages made by both of their daughters. They had held particularly high hopes for Peter's mother, whose excellent singing voice they were keen to translate into an advantageous contract, but, with typical stubbornness, their younger daughter had chosen to fall in love with a penniless tailor, albeit one with undeniable talent and some ambition. Apparently, by the time this unfortunate betrothal was made public, their elder daughter had already removed herself to the country and married a man who had, somewhat optimistically, styled himself as the proprietor of a country estate.

Peter's father reminded him that his mother's parents had died within weeks of each other from typhus—the disease having clearly travelled from one to the other. A few years after their parents' death, the sisters decided they should try a family reconciliation, and so Peter's mother and father, together with their five-year-old son, travelled out to the farm for a 'holiday' which proved unsatisfactory to both hosts and visitors alike. According to Peter's father, in the wake of this brief visit a rift grew between the sisters, which made it even more surprising that Maria was now choosing to dispatch their son into the safekeeping of the sister from whom she remained estranged. Peter listened closely as his puzzled father tried to explain what his troubled wife might be thinking, but father and son both knew that, of late, his mother's mind and her memory had become unruly. Eventually, his father stopped talking, but instead of suggesting that he was going to prevent this calamity from happening, the downcast man simply urged Peter to go and be safe in the country, for perhaps his mother was right; things were likely to become more difficult in the town. Peter wanted his father to say more, and to elaborate on what he meant by 'difficult'; he wanted him to share, to treat him like a young man, but his father smiled nervously. 'You won't have to stay there forever. When things change you will return and continue with your studies.' There was a long silence before his father reached over a large bolt of cloth and placed a gentle hand on top of his son's. 'You will come back, Peter. And I'll be waiting for you. I promise you; things will be different then.'

YEARS LATER, when Peter walked into the cheerless Notting Hill pub and saw Victor sweeping the floor, he was sure that he recognized an earlier version of himself. A lonely man adrift in the world, who didn't yet understand how vulnerable he was. He immediately decided that it would be his responsibility to set about assisting this poor coloured immigrant to get on his feet and help him begin to make something of himself. Peter went back to the office and told Ruth that he had found the right man to help out with the business. 'Some of these coloured chaps are quite curious, aren't they, but this one is different.' Ruth stopped clacking away at the typewriter and looked up at him. 'Remember', he reminded her, 'if we're kind to people then people will be kind to us, and that's the truth of it, my dear.' Peter was sure that his father would have approved; even though Peter was trading in bricks and mortar, as opposed to tailoring clothes, the principles remained the same. Be open and generous, for there was no rule against making money and at the same time helping others.

Having heard this lecture before, Ruth now moved the papers around on her desk in an effort to look busy, but there was a singular determination about Peter's desire to recruit this West Indian man, so she asked him the question that was on her mind. 'I'm happy for you, Peter, but are you sure you haven't just made him up?'

AFTER THE WAR, and his release from the displacement cen- tre in Germany, a still disoriented Peter slowly made his way to the coast, and then across the Channel to London, having decided to seek out the man at an address that his father's assistant, Simon, had given him. Peter eventually stood be- fore a short, spindly individual in a jewellery shop in the City. The nervous, almost emaciated man did not appear anything like the saviour that Peter had imagined. In fact, the fellow did not even share Peter's native tongue. When he spoke, the man's improbably high voice made little dips and rises as he tried to affect a familiarity with the English language. How- ever, the wry smile on the jeweller's face suggested an over- whelming sense of pity for the uneasy, stubby-fingered young man in ill-fitting second-hand clothes who had recently ar- rived from the Continent. Peter shuffled nervously, and when the thin man extended his hand and offered the refugee em- ployment, Peter admitted to having no knowledge of the jewellery trade. After his first week, which was largely spent both delivering and picking up orders and supplies, Peter's employer took him to one side and spoke to him in an urgent whisper. 'Piotr, you must change your name. Believe me, the English, they do not want to work with Piotr.' That same day, he became 'Peter', which didn't seem to alleviate any of the hostility that he routinely suffered, but Peter grew fond of the jeweller, who, one afternoon towards the end of the summer, asked him to stay behind in the shop.

When everybody had left, the man asked Peter what he wished to do with his life. Peter blinked hard, for, since arriving in England, it was a question he was continually asking himself, but he had failed to come up with an adequate answer. The fearful journey out of the camp, and then across what remained of his country, towards Germany, had been harrowing. At the conclusion of his pilgrimage, it was clear to Peter that he didn't have a country to go back to, and he certainly no longer had any family. But having finally made his way to England, hardly a day passed without Peter wondering if he *really* did want to make a new life for himself in this gloomy and frequently unfriendly country. Each morning he travelled from his bleak East End hostel to the jeweller's, and on the weekend, he made a regular visit to a house of pleasure in Bethnal Green where he stood quietly in a queue with a dozen or so other men. This was now his life. Sometimes it might take an hour before he reached the head of the line, but after waiting a few moments for the lady to rearrange herself, he would knock and enter. Five or ten minutes later, a disappointed Peter would yank up his trousers, smooth down his clothes, and leave behind a disconcerted, untouched woman. Later, after a soft drink in a pub that welcomed his people, he would walk back to the hostel and ask the proprietor if he had finished with his newspaper. Alone in his room, Peter would read, and practice words, and in this way continue the process of improving himself. But for what reason he was still unsure.

WHEN RUTH FIRST ARRIVED at the secretarial college, the po-faced individual behind the desk asked if she had anywhere to stay. She posed the question without looking up in Ruth's direction, which irritated her, so she waited until the receptionist looked at her over the top of her spectacles. 'Well', the woman persisted. 'Do you have an address?' The college had promised her form mistress, Miss Simpson, that they would take care of finding her some accommodation, and even pay for the first month of rent, but her father had told Ruth that he didn't believe a word of it. He had given his daughter a five-pound note and told her that if she didn't like where the college put her then she should demand to be housed elsewhere, but not, he begged her, with the kind of loose-living lot who he had heard populated the capital. However, as it turned out, the rooming house that the college placed her in at Harrow-on-the-Hill was just fine.

There were five other girls from the college staying at the house, each of whom had their own room. She met them on her first morning in the main classroom, where they were all seated in two neat columns and waiting patiently for their typing instructions. Her housemates let her know that last night they had heard her being shown around by the landlord, but they had thought it best to leave her to get established. At the mention of the landlord, they all got a strange look in their eyes, as though they were anticipating some reaction from her, but she had already guessed what they were waiting to hear. Mr Pugh hadn't said anything untoward to her, nor had he done anything wrong, but from the moment he opened the front door she could tell that this lecherous man was sizing her up. At lunchtime, Audrey offered her a cigarette, which she declined, but Ruth watched as her new friend lit up with a carefully manufactured extravagance. 'Sleazebag, he is. More hands than a bloody octopus.' While each morning gawky Ruth was still struggling to tame her hair with a variety of clips and pins, she could tell that Audrey was drowning in self-control; she was the kind of girl who nonchalantly pressed eau-de-cologne on the corner of a handkerchief and then dabbed the scent behind her ears. That night, Ruth intended to write to her father and let him know that the house was clean and the rooms well-lit, but she chose instead to go to the pub with her housemates and sip on a port and lemon while her new friends giggled and flirted with the lads on the next table. Ruth sized up the suitors and quickly concluded that the young men were brave enough to engage in banter but, as far as she could tell, they were not able to take either the girls or themselves seriously enough to embark on a proper conversation. To Ruth's mind, the lads were a waste of time.

A few weeks later, Ruth found herself knocking on the hallway door to Mr Pugh's flat and announcing that she would be moving out. A chubby man with an owlish face named Peter Feldman had rolled up at the college in his flash car and he had quickly taken a shine to Ruth. She agreed to help him out with his business, but once she ran her eyes over his Notting Hill basement office, she could immediately tell that whoever he had employed before was a joke, for the letters on file were full of crossings out, heavily scribbled insertions, and incorrect spelling. What's more, she had to ask Mr Feldman to buy new typing ribbons and some lumpy Plasticine to clean the typewriter keys. Before too long her working hours began to increase, and the commute between Notting Hill and Harrow became difficult for Ruth to manage. As soon as Peter suggested that Ruth might want to give up college and work full-time with him, she jumped at the opportunity. Peter moved Ruth into a spacious ground-floor room near the office and assured her that she would be under no obligation to pay any rent. As his secretary, she would receive four pounds a week and he would expect her to be on call Monday through Friday, keeping the books in order and typing up the communication. Peter promised her that if she ever became disenchanted then she would be free to leave and return to college, and this was to be their arrangement.

Inside herself, Ruth felt relieved, for the nature of this 'arrangement' meant that she would most likely never again have to contemplate returning to south Yorkshire. When Ruth told the girls at the college, it horrified them that she was ready to throw in her lot with a stranger, but Ruth knew that she was finished with studying. After all, what was she really learning? She could already type after a fashion, and although she didn't know shorthand, Ruth assumed that this was something she could pick up later. Also, she had begun to suspect that the college was doing little more than training young girls to become compliant women in cardigans and voluminous skirts who, for three or four decades, would sit all day in outer offices, rattling the keys and listening to little bells ringing as they pushed their carriages back to the left, while exercising a nervous vigilance over who had, or hadn't, made an appointment with their boss. So, with Peter's blessing, Ruth happily stopped attending college, although, in the end, she regretted leaving without saying a proper 'cheerio' to Audrey or any of the other girls.

Once Ruth gave up her studies, Peter found sufficient work for her to do around the office, and then he started to walk Ruth back to her room after their evening 'cocktail' at the pub. To begin with it was just, 'Goodnight, pet', and a kiss on the cheek, and Ruth would stand on the pavement and watch Peter waddle off in search of his blue Jaguar. Then one night, more out of curiosity than anything else, Ruth asked Peter to come in for a drink, and she allowed him to take off his shoes and make himself at home, sensing that his company might go some way to helping her feel less lonely. After Ruth fell asleep, Peter lay next to her on the bed with his eyes open, staring at the ceiling. How on earth was he going to solve this problem? The girl was young, she was pretty, and, as he suspected, she was not innocent in the ways of the world. He had enjoyed watching her slowly unstrapping her bra, in part because the girl knew exactly what she was doing. An attachment was not something that he had bargained for but, having disturbed Ruth, Peter now felt responsible for her. The following morning, Peter dressed quickly. After kissing his sleeping employee on the forehead, he left the room before it was light and drove the short distance to his own flat. Peter knew that he had to do the right thing. That afternoon, instead of going for cocktails, and without asking Ruth what she wanted, he moved them both into a three-bedroom house on Westbourne Park Road.

Both the house and the basement flat were empty, for he had not yet rented them out, and now he would not be doing so. The honourable thing would be for Ruth to now live with him, but as what he was not yet sure.

At work, Peter began to teach Ruth the proper way to answer the telephone, and how to write and place ads for vacant flats in newsagents' windows. They gave newspapers a wide berth, for Peter insisted they were a waste of money. People looked in windows, and what they couldn't find in windows they discovered by word of mouth, that's how the business operated. He taught Ruth to be respectful to all the customers, although he could see that politeness was already a part of her nature. It was clear that Ruth understood that the neighbourhood was full of queers, tarts, and immigrants, and she couldn't have failed to notice that a great number of Peter's tenants were coloureds or working girls, but it was apparent to Peter that not for a moment did his new secretary feel inclined to look down her nose at anyone. When Peter was sure of Ruth's role in his office, he started to take her with him to look at houses that he might buy, and then he invited her to join him as he made the rounds of the local second-hand furniture shops, where he searched for tables and chairs with which he might furnish his properties. Suddenly, to a whole range of Peter's professional acquaintances, she became 'Miss Ruth', and at the end of the day, after they had locked up the office and been for a cocktail together, they would drive back to the house in Peter's blue Jag. Peter would ask, 'Is Miss Ruth happy?' He would laugh and continue to tease her. 'Is there anything I can do for Miss Ruth?' But Peter need not have worried, for Miss Ruth was settling into her new situation and trying to be content and grateful. Then Mildred, one of the more talkative of his tenants, and somebody who seemed proud of the fact that she used to do some modelling 'up the West End', began to show up at the basement office and hang around for a bit of 'girl chat' with Ruth, which didn't please Peter.

Although Ruth tried not to listen to Mildred, she couldn't prevent the woman from putting ideas into her head. Eventually, Ruth found herself thinking about what Mildred referred to as a 'sparkler'. 'Come on, love, he's got the cash. He's one of those fellars that come from the wrong side of the Bible. They're all loaded, and you don't want people thinking you're that sort of girl, do you? If there's no kiddie then tie him down with a sparkler.'

Ruth had noticed that, of late, Mildred was now timing her visits to the office to coincide with when she thought Peter might be out.

'Mind you, even if he gets you a ring, there's no guarantee that he's actually going to do the right thing and marry you. But at least you're on the right path. It lets people know, doesn't it?' Ruth, however, remained unconvinced that this was a path she wanted to follow. 'Go on,' said Mildred, 'be a bit saucy and talk to him about it. What's to lose? It's not like you'll be planning a big church do, is it? Ask him about a sparkler and a registry office wedding. It'll spook the fat bugger a little and he'll just settle for the sparkler, which is all you really want to begin with.' Ruth looked at Mildred, who was now blowing her nose with her eyes closed, a peculiar habit that always secured Ruth's attention. She knew Peter well enough to know that he would most likely do whatever it took to keep her happy, but it was Ruth's uncertainty regarding what *she* wanted that was causing her to be confused. The facts were, she was his secretary, and she was learning the property business, and she was meeting people; and, naturally, she had no thoughts of ever going back north. Rumour had it that Paul Hirst had gone off to Nottingham or someplace, chasing after a girl he'd met on a barge holiday. But what did Ruth really want? A sparkler? Or perhaps just a man who would actually reveal something about himself, *and* actually desire her?

AT LEAST TO BEGIN WITH, Peter did speak to her. He told her that he had learned to better himself during the years that he lived at an East End hostel and worked at a jeweller's. He was soon making enough money so that he could easily have afforded to move out and into a small flat, but he saw no reason to abandon the lonely proprietor on the front desk who would let him borrow his newspaper, for the fellow had come to regard Peter as a friend. 'It is important to be kind, Ruth, and I was being kind.' And Peter's kindness paid off, for it was this man, Bill, who suggested that on the west side of the city a man with Peter's charm might make money renting out rooms to the newcomers, some of whom had mistakenly found their way to the door of the hostel and had to be turned away. 'These people are desperate, and they have little understanding of this country, even less than you.' Bill laughed, and Peter tried to laugh along with him. 'You go over there, son, and continue to try and scrape some of the old country off your tongue, and I'm sure you'll make something of yourself.'

'Five years later, I had six houses divided into thirty rooms. I had a nice car and believe me, I looked after my tenants. But look at me now, I'm forty-two years old and the boss of more than thirty houses, all of them nicely divided up.' Peter leaned back on the pub's faux-velvet banquette and swept the air with his cigar as he said this, and Ruth watched as the burning ember traced a triumphant arc. He paused and lifted his orange juice, took a sip, and smiled. 'More than thirty houses, Ruth, and God knows how many rooms.' Peter propped his cigar against the edge of the ashtray, and then reached into his inside pocket and pulled out his wallet. With a delicate finger and thumb he slowly removed a creased photograph of a man and a woman standing together as though on their wedding day, and he held on tightly to the picture. 'This is all I have left to explain myself to myself. My parents.' He looked at the photograph, before turning it over as though there might be another image on the back. Then, without saying another word, he gently slid the photograph back into his wallet and Ruth understood that, at this particular moment, it was probably best not to ask any questions.

Sometimes Peter's recollections would surge, and he appeared to enjoy talking about himself. However, most of the time Ruth felt as though she was being held at a carefully calibrated distance. Once the photograph had been replaced, Ruth knew what would follow. The well-worn story of how he took Bill's advice and packed his suitcase and got off the tube at Notting Hill station and saw the migrants on street corners, cold and crestfallen and stamping their feet. They were unsure of what to do, and they had nowhere to shelter, as landlords consistently charged them exorbitant rents. And so, Peter's mind was made up. First, he secured a job with an estate agent in Shepherd's Bush; then later, he negotiated a loan from a landlord who liked the way Peter managed his building. With this money, Peter made a down payment on a house that had been condemned, but he was confident that the property would never see the wrecker's ball, for there was a housing shortage. That was how it worked. The local politicians would say one thing, but the forces of the market—'the real world, Ruth'—determined what actually happened. Peter laughed and asked Ruth if she wanted another cocktail, but she didn't. Two was enough. There was no need for him to try to get her drunk. What was the point? She hated it when Peter behaved as though he was full of himself, and he seemed to enjoy acting as though she belonged to him.

When Peter spoke to her like this, his words often came across as if they were part of a rehearsed narrative that he was prepared to share with anybody who would pay attention to him. His stories were presented as though every action on Peter's side was carried out with certitude, and without any need for self-questioning, and as she listened, Ruth could feel her confidence slipping away. Some evenings, after they got back from the pub, Peter would wriggle his feet into his slippers and then pour Ruth another drink and sit with her while they listened to classical music, although Ruth always made it clear that she preferred the television set. Peter smiled, but he was keen to establish a routine. His routine. During the week, he expected Ruth to work with him at the basement office, and at the weekends she cooked and cleaned. Peter imagined that Ruth thought of him as a benevolent, giving man. After all, his desire to befriend coloured people was all the proof that anyone could ever need that he was considerate. What more could a girl want in a man except maybe a bit of the other on a regular basis, but he could sense that Ruth was increasingly upset by the fact that he wasn't interested in that with her. He imagined that to start with Ruth might have been relieved that he had seen something in her besides the obvious, but occasionally the young girl would press him to articulate what exactly he did see in her. Peter, of course, found it difficult to discover the right words and, much to Ruth's visible disappointment, it was at this juncture that he always fell silent.

Naturally, during the two years that the pair of them worked together with Victor, never once were Peter's 'cocktails' really cocktails. Peter would buy a pint of bitter for his rent collector, a port and lemon for Ruth, and he was always content with an orange juice or some other soft drink. However, Peter always called these drinks 'cocktails', carefully dividing the word into two distinct syllables. As they huddled together at Peter's familiar table in the corner of the noisy Elgin Arms, Peter would encourage his guests to raise and clink their glasses before taking their initial sips, and then he would ask, 'Well, friends, what shall we three talk about to-day?' This was Peter's customary opening line, as he unwittingly played the part of a professor making small talk with a gathering of students. But Peter never gave his students a chance to answer, for he would launch quickly into a story about something that had happened earlier in the day. Perhaps the infuriating chap who was supposed to clean his Jaguar had not turned up, or maybe the purchase of a new house in Queensgate had fallen through because the sitting tenants had still to be 'persuaded' to move out. And then a breathless Peter would laugh loudly and drop a proprietorial hand on to Ruth's knee, and she might smile. Victor would avert his eyes and continue to sip quietly at his pint and wait for Peter's teasing to begin. 'Has my fellow orphan got anything to say?' But Victor understood that nothing was meant by the gentle teasing, for this was simply Peter's way of dealing with the difficulty of Victor's reluctance to speak. Eventually, Peter would stand up and rub his hands together. 'Okay, my sweethearts, some more cocktails, yes?' Ruth would watch as Peter trudged his lonely way across the soiled carpet towards the bar and, with increasing regularity, she would find herself wondering if Peter had any real friends.

BACK THEN, respectable English girls didn't talk to coloured men in pubs. Surely Peter understood this. No matter how much Peter wanted to make this man feel comfortable, leaving them together while he went to the bar to get more 'cocktails' was only going to get tongues wagging. Yet Peter kept doing this, but Ruth was too ashamed to raise the question of her feelings with Peter. She had recently found herself being followed in the street, on successive days, by a mahogany-faced suitor, who got close enough to her that she could tell that the man needed both deodorant and moisturizer. He said nothing, and after two days he disappeared, but the encounter had left her shaken. These days, Ruth had begun to notice English girls in the streets pushing their half-caste babies in prams. Of course, she didn't need to bother to look for the evidence of caramel skin, for the impulse to disguise woolly hair with big hats said everything. These girls walked uneasily, knowing full well that people were more than ready to spit in their faces. Even respectable men and women would give such women a mouthful, and then cross the road and move on their way. She felt sorry for the mothers, but she was conflicted. Part of her wanted to ask them what on earth they thought they were playing at, but she had an equally strong impulse to walk with them in the hope that the bullies might back off when faced with two women instead of one. But Ruth did nothing, and she just looked at the women out of the corners of her eyes and tried to imagine their lives. At night in the pub, she fell into the habit of holding on to Peter's arm whenever they both sat together with Victor, and then she would list a little in Peter's direction.

WHEN VICTOR WALKED into Peter's basement office to begin his first day of work, he was determined that he would not meet Ruth's eyes. He remembered what the ship's captain had said to him about coloured men and women in England and, sure enough, within days of his arrival Victor realized that many of the fellars on the streets and in the pubs were simply busying themselves chasing after 'skirt'. As soon as a nice-looking thing in a short dress walked by, the men would instantly forget that they were in England to make something of their lives. However, Victor's discipline had kept him on the right path, and after Peter gave him the opportunity to come and work for him, Victor bought a new shirt and tie and jacket, and this was how he showed up on his first morning. Victor was determined to make the right impression and, as

ANOTHER MAN IN THE STREET 133

he waited for Peter to gather his things and lead the way out of the basement office, he continued to make sure that he didn't make any eye contact with the girl behind the desk.

Later, once Ruth understood that Victor also worked part-time for a local newspaper, she began to talk more freely with him in the privacy of the office. She would ask Victor about the stories he wrote, clearly using her curiosity about his newspaper work as an excuse to find out more about him. Victor told her about going to Waterloo Station to interview the trickle of people who were still arriving on the boat-trains, and how he would then follow-up and do the rounds of the YMCA hostels and talk to the coloured residents. Ruth asked him why he didn't ask questions of English people, and suggested that he should interview the vicar at the local church, as she understood that a lot of West Indians went to church. She claimed to have seen them on Sundays spilling in and out of the place, and so when Victor finished his rent-collecting round for the day, he went to see the vicar, and the man told him that he loved the singing of coloured people and their dashing clothes. He also loved their babies, and so Victor wrote a story, but when he shared it with Claude, his editor predictably enough just screwed up his face and continued to insist that English people had enough outlets where they were able to speak about whatever was on their minds, but the *News* should be a place reserved for coloured voices.

Claude picked up both pint glasses and looked quizzically at Victor.

'You ready for another drink?'

'I don't know if I should.'

Claude snorted and then sucked his teeth.

'Well, while you're thinking about it, I'll just get the same again.'

Victor watched Claude cross to the bar of the dreary Coach and Horses and place down both glasses. There were a lot of girls on Victor's rent-collecting round, and one or two among them had already hinted that when they didn't have the rent money, they could offer up something else. While these women went through the lamentable masquerade of searching in their handbags for the rent money, Victor stayed on the doorstep, but he tried to make these women feel at ease by being neither rude nor dismissive. But it was Peter's girl, Ruth, with her trim figure, and good manners, and inquisitive nature, who was continually on his mind, even though she had not given him any reason to hope for anything from her.

WHEN RUTH WAS LEAST EXPECTING IT, Peter got her a sparkler. He drove with gloved hands fixed firmly to the wheel and took her up to the West End in his Jag. Peter pulled up outside a swank restaurant, where he paid an overly solicitous attendant to park the car, but once they stepped inside, Ruth knew that Peter would never be able to properly look out for her, for he couldn't see the way people were gawping at her. She was too young, and her unstylish, porridge-coloured clothes were a mistake. As far as Ruth was concerned, clumsy, overweight Peter seemed equally out of place, but he didn't seem to notice that he too was an object of curiosity. Peter waited until the waiter left them alone with the ice bucket and the bottle of champagne sticking out of the top, and then he plucked the ring out of his pocket and pushed it across the table in a way that made it clear to Ruth that he was feeling quite pleased with himself. Ruth looked at the black box, but she didn't know what to do, so Peter spoke up. 'Aren't you going to look inside?' Ruth opened the box and then closed it again, and Peter leaned towards her and held her hand. 'Well, it's what you wanted, isn't it? This is what you've been hoping for, isn't it?'

Ruth stared at Peter, but over his shoulder she could see the man behind the bar pouring shots from a high angle. Once the food arrived, Peter ate quickly, his utensils clattering against the plate, and she thought about what Mildred had told her about men knowing sod all about anything south of a girl's belly button, and very little about what goes on in a woman's head. For some reason, as she ate, Ruth wanted to remind Peter that before she met him, she was a simple girl who had only ever worn flat heels, and she was still that girl. She looked across the table. Peter raised his eyes and quickly tried to replace his lugubrious face with a smile. Ruth had grown to notice that, whenever Peter thought nobody was looking, his face would often collapse into a grim-faced struggle with what she guessed was some form of anguish. In fact, Peter never really relaxed, probably, she thought, out of fear that his sad expression might take up permanent residence.

Later that night, as they lay in bed, Peter began to talk about a period in his life when he spent time on a farm with an aunt and an uncle, and then he mentioned a three-room apartment in a town, and Ruth listened. Peter was working his way backward through time, and although she couldn't follow everything that he was saying, at least he was talking. It was evident that this was Peter's life in another language, before England, but she knew that he was holding something back. As Peter continued to unspool his story, she realized that, as ever, his talking was merely a gesture, like a 'sparkler'. It was all too easy, and she began to feel angry with him, and so she spoke quietly without turning her head towards him.

'But what about your parents? Where do they live?'

Peter sat upright and stared at her as though genuinely hurt.

'But Ruth, what does it matter? We've got each other.'

She closed her eyes, for she could see it all too clearly now. A poor, insecure boy was permanently trapped inside the shell of a man that was Peter Feldman. As Peter continued to stare, Ruth could almost hear Peter's troubled heart beating uneasily in the semi-darkness. Sadly, as she listened, she could feel her own conflicted heart beginning to falter.

RUTH LEANS FORWARD on the chair beside Victor's hospital bed and looks at her empty ring finger where no sparkler is in sight. More than forty years have passed since she moved into Victor's cramped flat and took off Peter's ring. She dumped it into the bottom of her handbag, vowing that never again would she put another ring on that finger. These days, she has no idea where it is, but there have been moments across the years when she felt stupid for having misplaced it. At the very least she should have pawned the thing, for, after Victor lost his job on the newspaper, money has often been a real issue.

The Polish nurse breezes into the room and, as usual, insists that Ruth should go home and have a shower and a nap, as Victor is likely to be asleep for the rest of the afternoon. Ruth wants to ask Danuta what is really behind the doctor's decision that Victor can be discharged at the weekend, but she feels as though she has already taken up too much of the woman's time by enlisting her help in the fruitless search for Peter. It was only after the aggravating doctor scampered from the room that Ruth thought of all the questions that she should have asked him, but by then it was too late. Danuta picks up Victor's charts and looks closely at the machines, before scribbling down some numbers and then hooking the clipboard back over the end of the bed.

'Well,' she says, 'if you're staying do you want me to bring you a drink? Ginger ale? Some water, perhaps?'

Ruth shakes her head. 'I'll be fine. Honestly, I'll just sit here.'

She receives Danuta's familiar 'Please yourself' shrug and then watches as the young nurse pushes her plait back under her cap and prepares to swish out through the curtains. But before Danuta does so the woman stops, as though she has forgotten to say something. She half-turns towards Ruth. 'You know you will have to make a bedroom downstairs for him. He will not be able to manage the stairs. Did the doctor say anything to you about this?' Ruth shakes her head. 'Well, this way it will be easier for him.'

As Danuta leaves the room, a flustered Ruth stares at the woman's back. A bedroom downstairs? Not be able to manage the stairs? Again, she wonders what else the foolish man omitted to tell her. Seriously, why not talk to her? She's not feeble, but she realizes that this is how they all like to do it. All of them. They speak in a low, confidential tone, yet they studiously leave things out.

PETER BACKED FARTHER into the shadows and looked up at the building. He was afraid to cross the street and climb the stairs to the apartment, for he knew that other people were now resident in the property he had once called home. He felt undone and asked himself, what kind of life did he imagine he might be returning to? Even before he left for his aunt and uncle's farm, it had been understood that, because of the changing times, university studies would not be an option for Peter. However, standing on the street in this manner was a brutal reminder of how, during his absence, life in the town had deteriorated. He left his ghostly hiding place and carefully made his way to what used to be his father's shop, which still functioned as a tailor's. A man sat in the window mending a jacket. The man slowly lifted his eyes and noticed Peter staring at him. The look of alarm on poor Simon's face was such that Peter knew instinctively not to move but instead just wait. His father's elderly assistant stepped outside and looked all about himself before cautiously approaching. 'Why are you not in the countryside?' he hissed. 'You cannot stay here; you have to get away.' Peter explained that he saw little point in continuing to hide himself away on a farm while worrying himself sick about his parents. He had come to find his mother and father, but where were they? Had his parents been taken away, and if so to where; and who were the people in their three-room apartment? Simon's eyes darted all about and then, with a firm grip, he took hold of Peter's arm. 'Peter, please. You must be quiet.' Simon shook his head and then released Peter's arm. He reached into his trouser pocket and Peter watched as the man pulled out some paper and slowly scribbled down an address. He pressed the paper into Peter's hands. 'Please, Peter, you must leave, but do so under the cover of night. The man at this address in London, he can help you.' With this said, the terrified assistant turned on his heels and, without looking at Peter, began to dash back to the shop.

Simon had always been kind to him, but really, what use was kindness now? How was Peter supposed to travel to London? He had been given some hasty advice and a scribbled address, but Peter's situation remained the same. He was on his own. In fact, he had been on his own from the moment his mother instructed him to pack his clothes and books and put him on a train and sent him to her estranged sister in the countryside, while his father moved to one side and allowed this to happen. For nearly a year, Peter had been forced to live in a place where he soon learned that a gold necklace might be exchanged for six eggs, and he came to understand that a tree inside the house in December was called a Christmas tree. Last night, on the farm, Peter stood in front of a full-length mirror and reached for a towel. As he did so, he could see that the rolls of fat around his stomach no longer fully disappeared when he sucked his breath in. When he peered down towards his feet the skin around his chin folded into an untidy staircase that ceased to exist only when he once again looked upwards. He was changing. His country was changing. Now, as he looked about himself, he could see that the street remained empty, and he realized that life had deposited him at a crossroads. He could do as Simon had suggested and turn and attempt to flee, or he could press on towards danger and continue to search for his mother and father.

THE FIRST NIGHT Ruth moved into the small flat with him, Victor sensed that the young woman was consumed with guilt. Despite her boldness, it was clear that Ruth simply wasn't sure. How could she be? To be seen out together with him would be regarded as shameful, and they both knew what people were thinking. In the days that followed, Ruth would sometimes loop her arm through Victor's as they walked together, but at other times she pushed her hands deep into her pockets. Whatever Ruth chose to do, he tolerated it, for Victor knew that she had to find her own way towards him. When they lay together in bed, he would whisper and reassure Ruth that if she wanted his help, he would be there for her, but it was difficult to know what exactly he might do to support her. In the meantime, Victor suspected that Ruth's entrance into his world might make it easier for him to move on to the next stage of his professional life, and so there was now an additional reason why he should try to take care of brave young Ruth.

SHORTLY AFTER RUTH LEFT the letter for Peter, she saw him by Ladbroke Grove tube station, looking uncharacteristically grubby and downcast. She was immediately struck by the thought that Peter had most likely positioned himself on the busiest part of the street in the hope of running into her. As he moved in her direction, Peter dipped a hand into his pocket and withdrew a folded sheaf of papers. Then the thickset man thrust them in Ruth's direction.

'I'm sorry, I haven't put them in an envelope for you.' Ruth took the bundle from Peter's hand, and then she spoke without taking her eyes from his face.

'Have you been following me, Peter? And what's with the papers?'

Peter offered her a wan smile. 'The freehold deeds to your new house.' With this said, Peter bowed his head and then turned with an attempted flourish that didn't match the slow-paced solemnity of his demeanour. There was no longer a Jaguar for Peter to slide into, and as Ruth watched him move off down the street, she began to grasp the magnitude of what might be going on in this man's broken heart. There was no talk of going for a cocktail; there was no shriek of laughter. In fact, Peter was no longer speaking to her as though addressing a slightly idiotic child. He appeared to be resigned to the truth that he no longer had anything to offer her beyond the gift of a set of papers which would allow Ruth the luxury of a roof over her head.

IN THE EVENING, as Danuta suggested, Ruth begins the process of turning the living room into a bedroom. According to the nurse, once Victor returns home all strenuous activity, and not just climbing stairs, will need to be kept to an absolute minimum. Ruth sighs deeply as she sits on the settee and looks around the cluttered space, whose chaos suggests that an impromptu jumble sale is in progress. This task, which she thought might take an hour or two, is clearly going to take up the rest of the night. Ruth climbs to her feet and once again begins to rummage through the boxes that are full of clippings of Victor's old articles, and photographs of Victor with various minor celebrities. And then there are the Caribbean Media Award trophies, and the many certificates of merit that he and Claude have received for *West Indian News*. Over the years, she has talked to Victor about donating these materials to an institute of some kind, but the depression into which Victor sank after being let go by the national newspaper resulted in his never bothering to act on her suggestion. Ruth stirs herself and slowly begins to carry another box of Victor's archive upstairs to the bedroom and then, on her return journey, she brings down sheets, pillows, and blankets. However, it is always the trek upstairs that takes the longest, for the cardboard containers are heavy, and once she reaches the bedroom, she finds herself unable to resist sitting down and once again looking through the contents of each box in turn. The material represents the evidence of Victor's life before things went wrong. Before the move to Fleet Street. Before Victor found himself out of his depth. She closes her eyes as she remembers how dejection took hold of Victor, and the drinking began to spiral out of control. Victor would sit around the house all day, reading the tabloid newspapers and listening to annoying light music on BBC Radio 2. His slurred speech fell into a pattern of repetitive clichés on the theme of how life is an adventure, and it doesn't come with a map, and at night Victor would toss and turn in bed, so neither of them got much sleep. Eventually, he began to pass through the storm, but it wasn't the same man who emerged on the other side. Victor was a quieter, more guilt-ridden person, but Ruth couldn't banish her suspicion that her mere presence in his life somehow embarrassed him, and contributed to his behaving so awkwardly.

As Ruth prepares herself for bed, and towels off her damp face, she lets her imagination drift. She wonders, will her daughter grow to look something like her as she pushes further into middle age, or will Lucy take on her father's features? And then she once again finds herself thinking about Peter. He knew there was a child, but Peter never showed any interest in Lucy. He never asked Ruth if she wanted to contact a lawyer to see if it might be possible to get Lucy back, but this suited Ruth, for she didn't want Peter to feel as though it was all right for them to be always talking about her mess, and the skeletons in *her* closet. Her mean-spirited mother. Her browbeaten, rather prickly father. Her loser boyfriend, Paul. She had lost count of the number of times she had asked Peter about his family and where he grew up. How did he come to be in England? He was a Jew. She knew this, but she didn't really know what this meant, other than some people didn't like them. But why wouldn't Peter talk about Jews? Did his being one of them account for his weird tastes? Is this why he just liked to look at her in her underwear, but not lay a finger on her? Whenever she questioned him about his lack of interest in her body, Peter would shrug his shoulders as if puzzled as to why this might be a problem for her, but he knew full well that he shouldn't be treating her in this fashion.

Ruth lies in bed and the reality fully dawns on her that, in the next day or so, Victor will be coming back to this house. She also understands that it is unlikely she will see Lucy again any time soon. During her daughter's surprise visit, she should have admitted that she knew she had wronged Peter. Nobody could blame her for having had a change of heart, but she should have made some effort to explain things to Peter. As Ruth stares at the ceiling, her thoughts begin to tumble in all directions. But it isn't her fault that one day Peter just disappeared. All she was trying to do was move on with her life. Perhaps she should have told Lucy that when she confessed the truth to Victor about having a daughter, Victor had no problem with this aspect of her past. So why, she wonders, does her child still find it so impossible to forgive her for being with Victor? Honestly, Lucy, he's just a coloured immigrant who has made some mistakes, but he's not done *you* any wrong.

Because Ruth didn't fall asleep until she could hear the birds twittering, she missed her regular seven o'clock bus. Ruth now finds herself standing at the bus stop with a group of strangers, all of whom look wide awake and irritated, as opposed to the sleepy, bleary-eyed crowd that she's used to. Danuta may have failed to track down Peter, but at some point, the nurse did suggest that maybe Peter had gone off to America. The same thought has crossed Ruth's mind, but she worries that to question Danuta further and ask, 'Why America?' might come over as pushy, so she has chosen to say nothing. The fact is, she isn't even sure of Peter's real name, which makes her feel stupid. Only two facts are really clear; one day Peter strolled into the college and offered her a new life, and then she abandoned him. Her duplicity apparently broke something in the poor man, who was evidently not as savvy as he liked to give off. But how was she supposed to know that he would turn out to be such a fragile soul? In the distance, she sees the bus moving away from the stop down the road, and people begin to jostle to make sure that they don't lose their place in the queue. Ruth closes her eyes and sighs, for she is now convinced that she needs to redouble her efforts to find Peter and make amends. She needs to tell him about her life after she'd turned her back on him and ask for his forgiveness. Clearly, it's about time she tried to put matters right instead of just floating along on a cloud of self-pity. As the bus shudders to a halt at the stop, Ruth feels impatient bodies pressing hard against her. It occurs to her that perhaps both Peter's and Victor's legacies to her have been to encourage her to think of herself only in terms of their lives. They both consistently neglected to ask how *she* might be feeling at any given moment, but she harbours no anger towards them because of their disregard. After all, twice now, she has willingly walked away from herself, and it's simply too easy to put all the blame on both of these men.

Ruth gets off the bus at the stop before the hospital. She crosses over to the other side of the road and begins to move quickly towards the tube station. One morning, not long after she began sneaking off to Victor's flat at every opportunity, Peter shuffled into the office and presented himself at her desk. Peter sheepishly handed her a scruffy piece of notepaper with a name and address scrawled on it. 'That's where I went when I first arrived in England. If anything happens to me, you can always go there and see this man. He's a jeweller.' And, of course, when something did happen to Peter and he completely disappeared, Ruth felt too ashamed to seek out Peter's jeweller friend. Given her behaviour towards Peter, why would anybody want to help her by answering her questions? Yesterday evening, she found the old, yellowing piece of notepaper in one of the many boxes of papers and clippings that she had slowly hauled up to the bedroom. She pushed the notepaper into her purse.

Ruth takes the train east and gets off at Moorgate, where she carefully follows the maze of streets to the scribbled address. This part of London is no longer a hotch-potch of narrow, smog-filled alleyways. The area is dotted with tall concrete and glass buildings, places where busy men and women in suits charge purposefully about in all directions. Number 273 is no longer a jeweller's shop. In fact, it is clear that this smart new office block has never hosted any such business. Through the plate-glass window, Ruth can see two uniformed men behind a reception desk, and between her and them there is a door-shaped metal detector through which everyone is expected to pass. Ruth creates a visor with her hand, and squints because she can see her own reflection in the window. She is an ageing woman, trying in vain to find some sign of a man she let go over four decades earlier, and this is where Peter told her to look. And now, here she is searching for him, but there is no longer any trace of Peter, or his former life, and she is merely staring at her own sad reflection.

Ruth carries her drink into a nice dark corner of the City pub and finds a seat by the window where she can look at the passers-by going about their affairs. Outside, she sees a solitary pigeon strutting along the pavement and cocking its head at the traffic. The pedestrians seem to be unaware of the homeless man who has decided to make a bed out of a piece of cardboard and position himself so they have little choice but to step around him. The last time Ruth saw Peter, he was waiting for her in the street as she was making her way back to the house which she now shared with Victor. Ruth was struggling with a heavy grocery bag, and Peter suddenly stepped out of a doorway and blocked her path. Had any other man done this it would have been an aggressive gesture, and she might have screamed, but Ruth could immediately detect sadness on Peter's face.

'I'm sorry, but I didn't know how else to get in touch with you. Since I gave you the deeds to the house you haven't answered any of my letters.'

Ruth sighed, startled to see Peter in this destitute condition. 'Peter, this isn't the time or the place.'

He smiled. 'Then maybe we should go for a cocktail?'

Ruth shook her head. 'Peter, please.'

'I didn't see it coming, Ruth. Not with him.'

'What do you mean?' Peter wouldn't meet her eyes, and so Ruth continued. 'What do you mean, "not with him"?'

'I didn't mean it to sound like that.' He paused. 'Ruth, you know what I mean.'

She stared at Peter, with his grubby collar and badly knotted tie that was not fastened up all the way. What had happened to Peter's money? To his car? She had read in the papers that the investigation into his practices had finished him off as a landlord, but the police had decided not to prosecute.

'It's not right, Peter. I can't talk to you here, you know that.'

'Then where can you talk to me?' He stared directly at her. 'Don't you think you owe me that much?'

Ruth looked at Peter and tried to add up in her head what she might owe him. He had given her a job and a place to live. But even now, she had no real understanding of what she meant to Peter. With Victor, it was different. Although he pretended otherwise, Victor needed her help, and not just with his research. She tried to smile at Peter, whose eyes were now beginning to well with tears. Then, without saying another word, Peter stepped to the side and cleared the pavement, allowing her to pass.

'Goodbye, Peter.'

Ruth regripped the heavy shopping bag and began to walk away. She didn't turn around, but she knew that until she crossed the street and passed out of sight, Peter wouldn't move. He would stand and watch her.

Ruth guesses that if Peter is still alive he must now be well over eighty. She makes the effort to imagine what he might look like, but it is a task that is too difficult. Ruth continues to stare idly out the window of the pub at the sea of humanity washing by in both directions, and she tries, in vain, to switch off her memories. But really, when you get right down to it, who had done the abandoning? It's not like Peter ever made any real attempt to treat her like a woman. But did it really matter who was to blame? Who among us knows what the truth is in any situation? When Charlie's letter plopped through the letterbox, claiming that after what Victor had put him through, he'd had to scarper out of the country—to Australia—she stood by Victor's side. Charlie said he wanted money or else he'd go to the papers, but Victor laughed scornfully and refused to pay up. 'If I'd done him any wrong, why would the man turn over his bedsit to me when he left for Australia? The man is talking bullshit.' Ruth chose not to turn her back on Victor. Peter had taught her well. 'People will say anything to bring you down. You need your friends to be loyal, Ruth love. You need your friends by your side.' But look at how she treated Peter. The one time that Peter opened up a little, and offered her some insight into his past, she showed no mercy. 'You went to a camp and nearly died? Then you escaped at the end of war and came to England? Escaped from where? What camp? Jesus Christ, I presume you're not talking about some holiday camp at Skegness or Filey? For Christ's sake, what are you on about?' But then later, after she had educated herself at the borough library, and then watched a documentary programme on the television about the war, she understood a little better. Of course, by then, Peter had long since disappeared. She should have been more considerate and patient with Peter, she understands this now. After all, having learned something about what he must have been through, she now accepts that Peter probably *couldn't* go back to the past in his head.

Peter was a kind man and, apart from his silence, he didn't do her any wrong. After the television programme Ruth couldn't sleep, for she kept wondering what it must have been like to become a man in a place like that. For heaven's sake, what did he see? What did he do? It was now clear to her that his urges must have turned squiffy there, but it pained her to dwell on the unpleasantness of her selfish decision to choose

Victor over him. The truth is, she needed to be touched. She takes another sip of her drink. She was hungry for attention. Ruth is ashamed because she knows that, in addition to yearning to experience a man's hands once again on her body, she also wanted to feel that she had something to offer. To her mind, abandoning silent Peter was a small price to pay in order to try and turn the spotlight on herself for a minute. As Ruth continues to look out the pub window at the lively City street, she now grasps that there's a vast difference between the 'can't say' of Peter and the 'won't say' of Victor. Mr 'can't say' gave her everything he could, but he just couldn't open the door to himself. Presumably, this would have meant Peter having to face up to a part of his life that he couldn't revisit. As for Victor, it is as though he's just been making it all up as he goes along. What dignity is there in just inventing a new story whenever it suits? Story by Victor Johnson. The past as inconvenience.

After a second port and lemon, Ruth decides to finish her drink and make her slow way back to the tube station and what will now be an early afternoon journey to the hospital. As Ruth leaves the pub, she looks around and imagines that everybody has probably lost something and needs some kind of help. My God, in her own small life she has lost sight of so much. Paul, the father of her child. Lost. Her child, Lucy. Lost. Peter. Lost. Even her mum and dad. Lost. But not Victor. He has a quality about him that has always made her believe that he needs her, even though his neglectful behaviour has often suggested otherwise. Furthermore, with Victor, for some reason, she has always found it difficult to become angry with him. As Ruth threads her way through the pedestrian traffic, she decides that this evening, once she gets back to her house, she will call Lucy and admit to her daughter that maybe she does need to leave Victor. Will Lucy please come and get her and take her back north before Victor is discharged from the hospital? Lucy, sweetheart, I need to sort myself out. Can you do this for me, love? Will you please come and get me?

AS THE TUBE TRAIN PREPARES TO STOP at her station, Ruth deliberately leaves the piece of notepaper, with the scribbled name and address, on the seat next to her. However, as she steps through the train doors, she hears the piercing voice of a young girl who is part of a gaggle of giggling teenagers wearing strappy dresses which reveal their tiny, sharp shoulder blades.

'Excuse me, missus, but you dropped this.'

The grinning girl, with a heavily ornamented stud in her nose, extends a hand and passes Ruth the scrap of paper.

'Thank you', says Ruth, offering the child a puckered smile.

'That's all right, missus.'

Ruth quickly tucks the notepaper into her bag and watches as the youngster hastens back to her seat, and the company of her friends. Once the Good Samaritan has rejoined her group, the girls begin to laugh anew. As they do, Ruth steps down onto the platform, the doors close, and the train begins to pull out of the station. Ruth turns in the direction of the escalator which she will ride to the top before emerging into daylight. Then she will walk carefully, but with new clarity, towards the red-brick hospital.

At the end of the afternoon, Ruth leaves Victor in the hospital and decides to make her way back home. She had sat with him and suggested that he might want to spend some time with his son, and then admitted that she really did need to see more of her daughter, but Victor looked hurt. They fell silent and she realized that, at this moment, she no longer had any words for Victor. As Ruth turns into her street, she can see Charlie standing across from the house staring blankly at her. She hurries inside and secretes herself in the kitchen, where she quietly makes herself a cup of tea. Then, after an hour, Ruth goes to the living room window and discreetly fingers back the net curtain. Charlie has now gone, but she imagines that he will return. Ruth passes back through to the kitchen, where she boils the kettle and then pours some hot water over a fresh tea bag. It is clear what she must do. After she has finished her new cup of tea, she will pick up the telephone. Ruth is ready now to seriously attempt to make peace with her foul-mouthed, sometimes drunken daughter, and perhaps she will be allowed to play some role in the lives of her two grandchildren. She is ready now to ask her child to forgive her for everything.

5 🌱

THE BOY UNDER THE BRIDGE

Y OU MEET A BOY when you are fifteen. He is the quietest boy in the village, and he doesn't appear to have many friends. It is clear to you that he needs somebody to draw him out of himself. All the girls talk about him; the silky way he walks, his broad, rounded shoulders, and his dark eyes, but the young man looks to the side of people, and seldom directly at them. Even when talking to somebody he knows, he averts his eyes. The other girls notice your interest and one by one they begin to move away from you. They are jealous and they cast you out, but as long as he might one day be interested in *you* then other people's feelings are not your concern. The young man leaves school and goes to work in the town helping in the office of the island newspaper. It is clear that he doesn't belong with the other men in the cane fields. However, come nightfall, he generally sits with these men outside the rum shop, but he simply listens because he's too shy to take part in their laughter and jokes. One night he leaves the men talking and, at your suggestion, he meets you under the bridge by the river. You sit and talk in the darkness, and eventually he confesses to you that he can never get any privacy in his parents' house. You tell him that he should get a place of his own, but he says he doesn't have the money. You meet a boy when you are fifteen and you hope that everything will always be this straightforward to you. Although you weren't able to name it then, one day you will look back and realize what you were feeling. You were feeling content. You were happy. Sitting with this young man night after night under the bridge by the river and watching him stealing glances at you.

SEX WITH HIM WAS A NATURAL THING. At first with the bare ground at your back, and then later, when he got his own small room to the rear of the piano teacher's house, you would lie still on his narrow mattress. His job now required him to also deliver newspapers around the island, so money was less of a problem and the shy young man felt happier. Sometimes, after he had finished, the pair of you would stare out the small window at the luminous shield of the moon and you wouldn't leave his room until it was morning. Some people just have sex, but you wondered if you might also discover love, so that sex and love might arrive like twins, but this didn't happen. He simply sexed you. You could feel the way people now looked at you, but you were equally dismissive in return. You didn't give a damn what anybody thought. What the young man wanted was the only thing that mattered; what he said was the only thing you listened to.

YOU WERE A GROWN WOMAN when he left you. You stood with your arms folded and made no effort to try to persuade him to stay. Why should you? He had been moving between you and the Englishwoman ever since you arrived in the country. He didn't deny anything. It was as though he was indifferent to his betrayal. England had hardened something in him. Back home, you had left school and gone to work for the civil service as an accounts clerk, and at weekends you attempted to make extra money by selling the raffia baskets that you wove from the delicate material of the palm tree. You hoped that one day he would ask you to join him in England, and after you finally made the passage, you signed up for evening classes and earned ordinary, then advanced, qualifications. You then attended the local teacher's college and received a teaching certificate, but it was too late. A desperate ambition had him in its grip. You couldn't keep up. What was the point of trying to keep up with somebody who could no longer see you? You stood with folded arms and saw the resigned look on his face as he started to stuff his clothes into a suitcase. Maybe the Englishwoman had given him an ultimatum? You asked him, 'What about our son?' He stopped, turned his head, and stared blankly in your direction. He had long ago exhausted any real interest in you, but you hoped that he still cared. However, as you watched him walk out the door, you reminded yourself that a person can also care about a cat or dog, but this thought didn't help. He was abandoning you, and you understood that your future was now behind you. You were by yourself. Alone. A school-teacher in England whose son was always gallivanting all over the place. You ate dinner by yourself in front of the television set and felt the full weight of the empty house. No doubt he thought he could go further in this world with a white woman on his arm. Plenty of them think this way. What exactly had you done to drive this man away? But it didn't matter now. The boy under the bridge had decided to set you down and leave you by yourself in England.

YOU TRY TO CARRY ON as normal. You let your colleagues know about your changed status, but you continue to bring up Victor's name in the staff room, as though your separation has not changed the nature of your relationship with your husband. Of course, people say nothing in response. They smile inanely as though the volume has simply been turned down on the conversation, and their blasted good manners annoy the hell out of you. Your teacher friend Raymond aside, your already limited social circle begins to shrink to nothing. In the evening, you continue to stay home and watch programmes about the upcoming marriage of Prince Charles to Lady Di, sometimes with your son, Leon, but more often than not by yourself. Soon after Victor took his leave, he wrote a letter to Leon. You saw the envelope on the doormat and picked it up and put it on the kitchen table. You imagine that father and son occasionally meet up and go for walks in the park, or just sit and talk at the house that Victor shares with the Englishwoman, but you have learned not to ask anything of Leon. You recently tried to persuade him to consider a sandwich course at the polytechnic, but he shrugged his shoulders, and you got the message. With your son, unlike your colleagues, you pretend that his father simply does not exist.

NANCY MORTON, the headteacher, calls you into her office and asks you to take a seat opposite her. The woman has a pair of reading glasses hanging from a thin chain that she wears around her neck. As you move towards her desk, you realize that the whole room has been carpeted into silence. You sit, fold your hands into your lap, and wait. As you are the only coloured teacher in the school, the woman often goes out of her way to be foolishly deferential. But today she gives you a dentist's smile and then comes straight to the point. Mr Dalton—Raymond—has spoken with her again. He alleges that, despite his making it clear that he wishes to maintain a strictly professional relationship, you continue to bombard him with messages. You say nothing, but Mrs Morton presses on and suggests you consider seeking some medical attention. A psychiatrist or therapist of some description. In fact, she has spoken to the school doctor about the situation, without mentioning your name, and she has a recommendation. The woman picks up a piece of paper from her desk, leans forward, and hands it to you. Nancy Morton now smiles pitifully. 'Lorna', she begins, 'you have about you a wounded quietness which is troubling to us. I know how difficult things must be, but we're all here to help.' However, there are only the two of you in the room, so what does she mean by 'we're all here to help'? And 'troubling to us'. People must have been talking about you behind your back. You look at grey-bunned, painfully deferential Nancy Morton and wonder who she goes home to at night. A new lady friend, now that Miss Hedges has left the school and retired to Guernsey? Or is she still dreaming about the young French *assistante* from Normandy whom she persuaded to stay on for another year before the beleaguered girl fled back across the Channel? This self-righteous bitch has no right to speak to you in this manner.

IN THE EVENING, you call Raymond's number, but when he answers you casually return the receiver to the cradle. Only a meeting in person can resolve this impasse. After all, it was he who, only a few weeks ago, first asked you out for a drink at the end of the teaching day, claiming that he would welcome some advice from you. He asked why you had made no attempt to get rid of your wretched West Indian accent and speak properly like the coloured newscasters. 'You would be so much easier to understand.' Privately you wanted to let him know that Victor had never expressed any problem with the way you spoke. Your country accent never offended his ears. In a hushed voice, Raymond announced that his marriage was 'on the rocks'. You watched as he nervously laced his fingers around the stem of the wine glass, and you recognized him as a weak man. However, because you were now on your own, and because you felt sorry for him, you allowed him to bed you. His excitement was childlike, and his moment of pleasure brief, but seemingly intense. Thereafter, you dressed quickly and hurried away from his semi-detached house before his wife arrived back from her estate agent's business. But the man misunderstood the nature of your arrangement. The next day, you stood together in the corner of the staff room. Raymond winked and touched your arm, and let you know that the 'one-off' was 'special', but he didn't seem to understand that, after just one assignation, he was not allowed to withdraw his affection. Raymond was unmistakably taken aback by your polite refusal to simply disappear. You watched the shoddy man mop his brow with a crumpled handkerchief like a pantomime villain. The following Monday morning you discovered Raymond's carefully composed note in your pigeonhole. He was attempting to draw matters to a conclusion, but the desperate man saw only a simple coloured woman who he hoped he might be able to let down gently. Poor Raymond had miscalculated, and now, some weeks later, the fool is trying to hide behind Nancy Morton. You think again about telephoning him and giving him a piece of your mind, but it's increasingly clear to you that, in a situation such as this, a face-to-face meeting is necessary.

THE FIRST TIME the police came looking for your son, you were sure they had turned up at the wrong house. 'You are looking for who?' Standing before you, the two officers seemed improbably young. The boy looked barely old enough to grow a beard, while the girl gawped unblinkingly as though she would rather be anywhere but on your doorstep. It occurred to you that perhaps their fellow officers had dispatched them to your house as an initiation joke. The boy spoke first. 'Leon Johnson. We just need to ask him a few questions, that's all.' You stared at the pair of them and wondered what on earth had made them choose policing as a job. Perhaps some careers teacher had pulled out a heavily fingered folder, handed them a leaflet, and encouraged them to take a look. He had no doubt offered them some vague advice about opportunities and pension plans, things they didn't even know they were supposed to be interested in, before ushering them out of his office. 'My son is not here. Perhaps you'd be kind enough to tell me what you want with him?' It was now the girl's turn to talk, and you realized that they probably trained them like this. First one speaks, then the other. 'We'd be grateful if you'd ask him to call in at the station when he gets back.' The girl smiled, which was an unfortunate development.

AT THE WEEKEND the clocks go back. The days are becoming uncomfortably short, and you spend a few chilly evenings staring blankly at the television screen as it flickers brightly in the corner. But you are neither watching nor listening, and you remain unsure what, if any, relationship the images bear to the words emanating from the set. Raymond continues to distance himself from you, but this one unresolved entanglement now constitutes the entirety of your social life. Your son comes and goes as he pleases, and whatever relationship he has with his father he chooses to keep hidden from you. You tell your son that the police were asking after him, but he seems untroubled by this news, only vexed that you should have allowed yourself to be the messenger. You decide not to mention the police again, but you remain concerned. For the first time you think seriously about selling up and going home. A returnee—a West Indian returnee—is what they call people like you, but after all this time in England who do you know? Over the years you have made no effort to keep in touch with people. You travelled to join Victor in London, where you soon learned to embrace the English routine of shop, cook, scrub, laundry, and every winter—get sick. You had to sort out a school for Leon, and then retrain and start a career, and support Victor in his life and work while struggling to accommodate the indignity of his Englishwoman. Who the hell had time to keep in touch with the past? Anyhow, nobody back home made any real effort to keep up with you. Not even a letter or postcard. That said, how would they have known where to find you? However, in the evenings, as you watch the television set illuminating the forlorn room, the thought of maybe one day leaving the country and beginning again, back home, momentarily lifts your spirits, even though you know you are trapped in England.

THE MORTON WOMAN won't stop pestering you, so you decide to make the effort and call the frigging therapist. Dr Wheeler asks if, now that he has you on the line, he might be allowed to do a brief phone consultation. Have you, he asks, considered getting a pet? He continues; non-human companionship is known to stimulate a wide section of one's emotional spectrum. You listen for a while before noisily hanging up.

YOU THINK ABOUT calling Victor to let him know that the police are looking for his son. However, you don't need to hear his voice asking you how you are. How do you think I am? You damn well humiliate me and run off with some Englishwoman. Frankly, if that's the kind of woman you wanted, then why ask us to come to England? You could have just sent money to help support the boy and we could have kept our backsides at home. Do you know how happy the boy was when he knew that he was finally going to meet his daddy in England? But that happiness didn't last any blasted time. One day, not long after we get here, the poor boy is looking fretful, and he asks me why nobody in England is smiling and I tell him straight that people in England can be worthless and they don't want to give off any conversation to low-grade people like us.

VICTOR'S IS AN UNNECESSARILY FORMAL LETTER. He asks if you might consider meeting up so that you can discuss Leon's future. Because the boy will soon be leaving school, Victor thinks it might help if you are both on the same page. He could have said all of this in a phone call, but there is an intimacy to speaking with you on the phone which he probably has no desire to experience. However, despite the damn stupid letter, he is still your husband. There has been no communication from a lawyer, although it's clear that you have been discarded. Since his departure, Victor has made matters worse by not allowing you the opportunity to put things right. In his letter, he is asking for a conversation, but not one that will address your marriage. Apparently, your husband only wishes to discuss your son's future.

THE POLICE COME BACK a second time, but you don't open the door. Since the Brixton riots you're in no doubt how the police treat single black women. You assume it's the same pair, and you hear a girl's voice shouting through the letterbox. 'Mrs Johnson, we just want to talk to you.' You hide behind the living room door and wait. The man takes over. 'Mrs Johnson, if you know where Leon is you should tell him that we just want to talk. He's not necessarily in any trouble.' You realize that Leon probably hasn't been spending any time with his father. In fact, you're sure that he's been getting up to no good with his so-called mates. You can hear your heart pounding, but you close your eyes and start to count to one hundred and hope that the two of them will soon leave you alone.

'Mrs Johnson?'

YOU START TO READ A BOOK about grief that you have taken out from the local library where, somewhat bizarrely, they have already decided to put up Christmas decorations. It is not even December. Tinsel streamers in a variety of metallic colours are neatly tacked up along the edge of every bookshelf, and a small tree stands incongruously on a three-legged table, whose surface is decorated with a muddled sequence of undulating stripes of tissue paper that have been laid out in the hope that they might represent a rainbow. The tree itself has been adorned with shiny red paper bells and two lonely sprigs of mistletoe. It's sad to think that somebody has expended so much energy to create so little cheer. The author of the book about grief suggests making a 'battle plan' for each day in a notebook that you should update every Sunday. Supposedly, one must be ready to conquer time with activities. But you don't knit, you don't really cook, you spend no time gardening, and you don't like to go for walks, as there has been a spate of muggings. Furthermore, you don't have any pen pals or a secret desire to learn a musical instrument. Strangely enough, you do have a desire to touch Victor's clothes and to move carefully in and around the space that he used to live in. You want to continue to sleep in his bed, and you want to believe that one day he will realize that he has made a huge mistake. But, as far as you can tell, the book about grief doesn't address these points.

HE LEFT YOU BEFORE—for over five years. One morning you both stood quietly before a court-appointed officer, who quickly married you without the fuss of a church or any family, and then the following week Victor boarded the ship for England, where he hoped to find a job and a place to live. He said you would be apart for a year, or two at the most, but he would write every week and in due course send for you. To begin with, his letters arrived regularly; he told you about the young English boys who dressed in long coats and who choked their legs into small trousers. He said he had found work labouring in a pub, and then he secured a job in the housing business, and he was also writing articles for a newspaper. He told you about the one time he went to the cinema, and how there was a break in the film and people started selling ice cream in the aisles, and then at the end of the picture everybody had to stand up for the national anthem. You told him you wanted to see a daffodil. 'I read about them at school, but I never see one.' Then the letters stopped arriving so frequently and you started to worry that maybe he had forgotten you. You waited with your son, who soon grew to be a talkative little boy. The two of you were living life as though sitting anxiously in a public waiting room, with everybody staring at you and thinking to themselves that *your* turn was never going to come. But eventually you let Victor know that if he wanted to see his son then he knew what he had to do. When he finally sent money and gave you permission to book your passage, you looked hard at everybody in the village, but there was no reason for you to say anything. It was clear what you thought of them, and equally clear what they thought of you. You left for England knowing in your heart that returning home was not going to be an option. There could be no return to these people. Or to your baby daughter. But what were you supposed to do? You couldn't take the girl with you and ask Victor to look out for another man's child. Your daughter's father would have to watch over her.

YOUR HUSBAND STILL HAS THE KEYS to the house, which has always been a source of some comfort to you. This means that Victor can come in at any time of the day or night. After he sent the cold letter asking if you might meet up and talk about Leon, you thought about drawing the bolt across the front door. You had no intention of replying to the letter, and you thought to yourself that maybe now was the right time to lock him out of your life. But then it struck you; what if Leon came back unexpectedly? If the bolt was drawn, how would your son get in the house? You sit in the armchair by the window and start to flick through the Yellow Pages looking for a locksmith. In future, only you and Leon will have possession of the keys to the house. It's probably time to face up to the upsetting truth of the situation, but your mind starts to drift. You don't want to lock Victor out. If he comes back into the house, you will most likely ask him something stupid like, what does he want for dinner? Or how was it at work? You will try to become a different kind of wife; one who is less angry and not so frustrated with him. You will pretend that nothing has happened, and that he has never been away at all. However, if you change the locks and force Victor to press the bell, or knock at the door, then you won't have the opportunity to show him things are now different. You slowly put down the Yellow Pages and then look out the window. There are a series of cloudy wisps in the sky. Of course, the sun isn't going to bother to come out today.

.

LEON HASN'T BEEN HOME for some weeks. Then, one evening, he calmly opens the door to the house and announces that he will be staying with you for a while, and you are grateful. You wait until the morning to ask him if he has spoken with the police, but you are careful to make it clear that you are not passing on any messages. You are not an intermediary. Leon shrugs and says that he's 'straightened everything out'. You breathe a long sigh of relief, and then worry that your sigh might have been audible. However, Leon continues to cram cereal into his mouth. You have already decided that you are not going to ask your son anything further. If there is anything else to be said then Leon will tell you in his own time. It will soon be Christmas.

ON LEON'S BIRTHDAY you bake a cake. When your son returns at the end of the day, you cut a slice and put it on a plate for him. He looks remorsefully at you, then picks up the slice of cake and takes a bite. 'I'm meeting Dad later', he says. 'We're going out for a pizza.' You smile at your son and say, 'That'll be nice.' Leon puts down the cake. 'Look, I don't have to go if you'd rather I stayed here.' Your son seems to sense your hurt, but the last thing you want is for him to take on your burden as his own. 'No, you must go, I'll be fine.' This is the first of the special days. Leon's birthday. Soon it will be Victor's birthday. Then later, your own birthday. You have no idea how you are going to make your way through these anniversaries, but baking cakes is not going to help lessen the pain.

LEON OCCASIONALLY MENTIONS his father's 'girlfriend', but the very word seems absurd. Calling her his 'woman friend' might make it easier to bear, but 'girlfriend' feels insulting. You understand that Leon wants you to move on. You know that your son also wants you to end your sick leave and go back to work, but you sense that it's still too soon. Maybe after Christmas, but not now. At night you continue to dream of Victor, and how you and he would meet under the bridge. In your imagination, the scenes that follow are joyful. After five years, a heartwarming reunion at Waterloo Station. Moving from a bedsit to a proper flat. Leon passing the eleven plus and you both taking him out for ice cream to celebrate his success. Putting down a deposit on a comfortable house with a big garden. Victor succeeding Claude as the editor of *Race Now* and insisting that the two of you go for a romantic dinner in the West End. Sending for your daughter to join you in England. But then you wake up and pray that you will never again be visited by such thoughts, for they only make your current plight harder to bear. It is a cold morning, and the radiators are not yet on. The thermostat is set for seven a.m., but it is only five a.m. It is too soon for the birds to sing. Too soon for light to start fingering its way into the bedroom. Still too soon to go back to school. Nancy Morton will have to continue to do without you.

YOU NEVER TOOK A HOLIDAY TOGETHER. Perhaps the problem was as simple as this. You never took time to be with each other without the day-to-day difficulties of making ends meet. But where would you have gone? To the English seaside? Brighton? Bournemouth? Sprawling on a beach and eating candy floss was too English for either of you. And neither of you spoke French or Spanish, nor did you have any desire to learn, and so why bother crossing the Channel?

People forget that holidays are not really an option for immigrants. One journey is enough. You're already on the biggest, and most permanent, *holiday* you can ever imagine. After this, anything else is a waste of time and money. But you wonder; maybe if you had just tried. A weekend together in a hotel room in Central London? Or an exciting trip to somewhere foreign, like Greece?

NANCY MORTON WRITES to let you know that Raymond has chosen to take early retirement. He and his wife are moving to the Algarve, where they will live out their golden years baking themselves in Portuguese sunshine. It is not a personal letter. The head teacher has sent a copy to everybody informing them of Mr Dalton's decision. ('Dear Members of Staff'.) It appears that Nancy Morton believes that the school will miss him greatly.

THE LAST NIGHT you spent with Victor, he climbed into bed after you. He eased both the sheet and covers up to his neck, leaned over in your direction, and whispered, 'Goodnight'. He did so quietly in case you were already asleep. Then he gave you his back. It had been like this for years, and neither one of you made any real effort to do anything about it.

IT IS CHRISTMAS DAY, and Leon has said that he will spend the morning with you; this way, you and he can have Christmas lunch together. Later, in the afternoon, Leon claims that he will go to his father's and spend the rest of the day there. It is difficult to know if Leon is lying, but you have your suspicions. Your child is growing into a tight-lipped stranger. You don't ask him if the 'girlfriend' is going to be present, but you assume she will be. Your son asks if you will be doing anything special, but you both know that he is just trying to make himself feel less guilty. When you go back to school in January, you have promised yourself, you will start to make more of an effort to become part of a community. You will also discard the hideous, ill-matched clothes that you have accustomed yourself to. But first you must survive Christmas Day. You have wrapped Leon's presents. You have decorated the Christmas tree. The turkey is ready to go into the oven. Even though you have not bothered to attend to your wild and untamed hair, you will be having an English Christmas with your son.

A RE-RUN of an old *Morecambe & Wise Christmas Special* has now finished. You turn off the television set and sit back down. You unscrew the bottle and arrange the pills in a straight line, like soldiers. Twenty-seven. You count them twice to make sure. Leon said he would probably stay overnight at his father's, if that was all right with you. You could have said, your father already has somebody to keep him company, so could you please come back and watch some television with me? But then your son might have asked, what about my sister? At this point you would have been forced to smile. Then explain. I can't tell you anything about your sister. I'm sorry. I'm not proud, but we left her behind

and made a new start in England with your father. You meet
a boy when you are fifteen. The other girls are jealous, and
they cast you out. Twenty-seven laid out in a straight line.
You hear the neighbours, Maurice and Elsie, knocking on
the front door and so you hide in the kitchen and pretend
that nobody is in. Shouldn't they be at home pulling Christmas crackers? Elsie pushes open the flap of the letter box.
'Lorna? Lorna, love, we've brought you some pudding. Is
everything all right?' Of course, everything is all right. Why
shouldn't it be? Leon and I are having a hell of a party. And
then later, after you are sure they've gone back next door, you
once again turn on the television set but decide to keep the
volume low.

IN THE MORNING, Elsie knocks again and then rings the
doorbell. 'Lorna!' You think, Oh, Jesus, what's the matter
with the damn woman? Then you roll over in bed. You look
up and you are once again reminded that the curtains won't
close properly because they are missing a few hooks. Three
hooks, you guess. Nobody can ever explain to you how you
should prepare yourself for life after abandonment. Once you
get over the shock, you inevitably find yourself drifting in
one direction as you are keen to remember—and then in another as you seek desperately to forget. Of course, you have
made the mistake of not creating any new memories which
might help you to leave behind the battleground of remembering and forgetting. Except for Raymond, that is. You
need to make new friends. Give yourself something to look
forward to. Discover a reason to wake up in the morning. But

you sense that people are always moving away from you; they are quick to smile and then they flee. It was like this when you were a girl. But then there was Victor. He listened to you. The boy under the bridge. But now you are a woman, and it is like this again with people always moving away from you. Some people will even go as far as Portugal. But this time there is no Victor. 'Lorna, love. Open the door.'

6 🖋

RUTH

VICTOR DIED AT TEN P.M. on a quiet Saturday evening. It was May 12, and so he avoided the mis-
fortune associated with the thirteenth, although
this wouldn't have worried him. Victor always used to insist
that he didn't possess a jot of superstition, but he once told
me that when he first came to England the people he worked
with took to calling him 'Lucky', which he found a bit odd.
However, typical of Victor, he didn't bother to correct them
or ask them to stop, he just went along with it and whatever
he was feeling inside he just kept to himself. Throughout the
dark, worry-filled hours of Friday night, it was just the two
of us alone, with me sitting on the plastic chair to the side of
his hospital bed and carefully holding his frail hand between
mine. The attentive West Indian sister, with her unlikely bob

of brown hair and outmoded horn-rimmed spectacles, fell into the habit of occasionally popping her head around the door and making an effort to smile. She would glance at the blinking lights on the monitor, and then wait for a beep which suggested that life was ongoing, before retreating and leaving the two of us alone. It was a noticeably distracted Danuta who came on duty on Saturday morning, but I was grateful to have another person around who was familiar with the pair of us. Later, at some point in the early evening, having noticed that Victor had fallen asleep, Danuta practically ordered me to go and get something to eat in the cafeteria, assuring me that the West Indian sister would keep an eye on him. Reluctantly, I climbed to my feet and left, but I still feel ashamed that when the end came, I was downstairs in the basement eating a sandwich, and not where I should have been.

When I think of it now, I also feel regretful that I never seemed to be able to remember the West Indian sister's name. However, during what turned out to be Victor's final weeks, I was permanently unsettled and not sleeping properly. It's hard to believe that only a short while earlier, before the diagnosis, Victor had been approaching life as though—this stupid Charlie business aside—nothing was amiss. He would sit at home listening to music on BBC Radio 2, or to people talking on Radio 4, and on Sunday he chose to relax with the *News of the World*, for it annoyed him the way all the fancier newspapers were splintering into sections. He'd say, 'You pay for one newspaper, and you get six papers and three magazines, which is crazy.' He had stopped hiding his grey hair beneath a trilby hat, but it was still neatly combed, although it was noticeable that Victor had started to use some kind of oil, for his hair had a spongy sheen and it was now slightly damp to the touch. Understandably, he was still disappointed with the way things had worked out for him, but I could see that Victor was now trying to tamp down any bitterness. His disposition was clearly lifted when the United States finally made a black man the president, but he never spoke to me about it. The idea of sharing his feelings with me remained something that Victor couldn't bring himself to do. Sadly, I continued to feel that I was an embarrassment, a mistake it was too late for him to rectify, and I had long given up on any hope of true affection, so I went along with the pretence that nothing was amiss. Together we talked idly about joining the Silver Seekers Fitness Club, and we paid for our senior discounted tickets at cinema matinees, and sometimes ventured out for dinner at the local Mediterranean restaurant at the ridiculously early hour of four thirty in the afternoon, often arriving before the staff had even managed to replace the lunch menus with the dinner cards. Victor didn't seem to care, and he even behaved with some zest, as though now that he was officially elderly he could do whatever he pleased. But all of this 'freedom' changed with the bad diagnosis.

Victor received his news on a chilly January morning, on what was supposed to be a routine visit to Outpatients. Having given us his grim verdict that Victor might have a year or two at best, the annoying doctor insisted that Victor should stay home next to his oxygen tanks, and he also instructed him to avoid any strenuous exercise. Did we have a car? No, I said, we didn't have a car. The doctor sighed and shook his head, and then his voice shed its professional concern and became somewhat bossy. He told us that a bus pass might be a blessing of the welfare state, but he advised us that the stress of getting on and off a bus, and finding a seat, and then alighting at the right stop, would be too much for Victor. In future, if we insisted on going out, we were to absorb the expense of taxi fares. We listened to the doctor for what seemed like forever, and I nodded silently and was pleased to see that I had left a messy red gash on the lip of the man's coffee cup. Meanwhile, Victor kept his perturbed eyes on the floor.

By February, Victor was hardly venturing beyond the sanctuary of our bed. There was a bathroom in the corridor just beyond the bedroom door, but it was my suggestion that I buy a potty, and I let Victor know that I'd happily empty it and wash it out to save him the trouble of trundling to and from the toilet with the paraphernalia of his newly upgraded, but still cumbersome, breathing equipment. At first the noise of urine cascading into the plastic vessel caused Victor to be mortified, but I told him that I'd read in one of those hospital waiting room leaflets that indignity often moves step by step with ageing, and I assured him that he would soon accustom himself to his new situation. But I needn't have bothered with my pep talk, for I could see that the reality of Victor's new predicament was beginning to undermine his spirit. His previous exuberance soon deserted him, and it clearly troubled Victor to find himself dependent upon me. However, Victor was fortunate, and he knew it, but as his situation worsened, he appeared genuinely taken aback that I might want to care for him, and his discomposure suggested that somewhere inside him he felt that he didn't deserve to be looked after. This state of baffled consternation stayed with him right to the end.

Early in the new year, around the time of the diagnosis, I was happy to discover that my daughter seemed open to speaking with me more regularly on the telephone, although our fumbling conversations were never easy and often collapsed into argument. Lucy had married well. Matthew was a schoolteacher who had a proper sense of responsibility, and their twin boys were being brought up so they wanted for nothing. However, Lucy was obviously determined that I shouldn't have anything to do with her kids, and she made it clear what she felt about Victor. It was some years now since my daughter had tracked me down, but having found me, Lucy never reconciled herself to the fact that she was expected to take Victor too. I told her that he had lied to me about his wife and child, but there was more to Lucy's disdain than just this. I could see what Lucy thought of me by the way she looked me up and down. After all, I'd had to endure years of 'that look', which had me pegged as a slag, so I didn't need my daughter to say anything. I could see it in her disappointed eyes, the same way that I saw it in Mildred's eyes when, after I stopped working for Peter, I went to let her know that my circumstances had changed. Mildred wasn't really a close friend, but once I moved in with Victor, and put Peter out of my life, I realized that I didn't really know anybody, so visiting with Mildred was pretty much a matter of needs must.

Because I used to do Peter's books, I knew that Mildred lived on the top floor of one of Peter's properties, a tall house whose decaying façade was decorated with huge, irregular patches where the plaster had become dislodged and fallen off. When I pressed the bell, Mildred's window flew open, and she poked her head out. 'What are you doing here?' Mildred didn't wait for an answer, she just flung down the key, which rattled to the ground at my feet. I let myself in and started to trudge up the squalid staircase, stopping at each landing to flick the light switches, which, predictably enough, didn't work.

'Well?' she said, as I looked around her small, dishevelled room. Mildred was leaning against a heavy chest of drawers, while her smalls were drying on a rack that had been placed next to a paraffin heater. The combination of the heater and her laundry created a musty atmosphere that was damp, almost wet. The two small windows to this attic room were filthy, and I could see that the wooden shutters were hopelessly misaligned and would never be able to close properly.

'I suppose you've come round here looking for a bit of a gossip, have you?'

I didn't know what to say so I stood before Mildred and started to straighten the rug with my foot. I watched as she struck a match and lit a cigarette.

'Look, love, I've always liked a natter with you, but Peter's in a bit of a state and I don't want him to think I'm being disloyal and then chuck me out.'

I nodded and said, 'I understand'. I moved as though I was going to leave, but Mildred practically shouted.

'Where do you think you're off to? Sit! You've only just got here.'

Mildred picked up some bras and a petticoat from the settee and then plonked herself down and directed me to sit beside her. 'Look', she began, 'you're a nice-looking young bit, so what did you go and do that for?' Her eyes were now boring into me in a way that made it difficult to separate pity from distaste. 'Come on, we both know what they say about them being able to entertain a girl more than an English bloke. Is that why you did it? I mean. Peter got you a sparkler, didn't he? I just don't understand you. Now people are just going to think you're a prossie, and we know you're not that sort of girl.'

For a moment, I wanted to open my mouth and protest, but I didn't see the point. Clearly, this woman had never really been my friend. In fact, she had no interest in listening to me, and I had absolutely no business being in her room. But what hurt the most was the way that she was looking at me, like I was a piece of dirt that had got stuck to the underside of her shoe.

Victor's bad diagnosis was already sapping the energy out of our lives when, in late February, the results of a new series of tests made this period even bleaker. What the doctor had suspected in January was now confirmed; Victor's lungs were ceasing to function, and the hospital had no choice but to admit him for further observation. His month-long spell in hospital ended abruptly when early one spring morning the nurses began to dress him in his own clothes. I was told that an ambulance would be provided to take him home, but nobody bothered to explain to either one of us why he was being suddenly discharged. Had they finished with all of their prodding and probing? Had they discovered something new that they didn't want to tell us about? I confronted a nurse on the ward, who grimaced at my raised voice before letting me know she'd be back in a minute. With this said, the woman walked off. There were six beds in the communal ward, and

Victor had been given one of the beds by the window that looked out onto the car park. It was not much of a view, but it was definitely better than having to stare at the other patients. I suspected that it was assumed that in exchange for this perk, we should be grateful and not make a fuss. But why should I show gratitude? And why now, when Victor was being sent home without any explanation. The portly West Indian sister appeared by Victor's bedside and put her hand on my upper arm just below where it met my shoulder. It was less than a grip, but more than a touch; enough for me to feel her concern, but also the right degree of pressure that might help me to register the gravity of her words. 'Mr Johnson should go home now, and the doctor will contact you. The ambulance will soon be here.' I stared into her placid face but understood that there was nothing to be gained by quizzing her for further information. 'Your husband needs to be made to feel comfortable.' She wasn't to know that we weren't married, but coloured women usually didn't use the term 'husband' with me when talking about Victor. I continued to stare at the sister, but my mind turned to the more practical problems of settling Victor back into our bedroom, and then once again setting up his breathing equipment and trying to encourage him to eat.

The following day the doctor telephoned us at home, and I put the call on the speaker. After being discharged from four long weeks in hospital, Victor had been cautiously optimistic that we might be in receipt of an improved prognosis. However, despite the doctor's mollifying tone, the news was sombre. At the end of the call, and in what was now becoming a familiar gravelly whisper, Victor spoke to me of his desire to, at all costs, keep the pain under control. After Victor finally agreed to take an afternoon nap, I tiptoed downstairs and made an appointment with the local GP and suggested that she get hold of Victor's records from the hospital, so that she would be in a position to answer my questions when I came in to see her. Dr Patel was from India, or Pakistan, I'm not sure which, but she was from that part of the world. She was also young, and for some reason always smelled of stale perfume, but she was capable. That's all I needed, somebody sensible to talk to in an open, genuine way about what was going on. Later that week, she kept glancing down at the hospital records spread out on her desk and then nodding as though discovering something new that she had hitherto not seen. I waited for her to bring up the idea of a care home, but Victor and I had discussed this and vowed to reject it should we be offered this as a possibility. Mercifully, Dr Patel steered clear of the subject, and I stared first at the blank wall behind her head, and then at the sad rack of magazines in the corner of the room, and wondered what Victor and I might do with the year, or maybe less, that I assumed we had left together. Hopefully, Dr Patel might help me to understand what was realistically possible in this situation. Little did I suspect that we were only talking about a few weeks.

One afternoon, in early April, I traipsed downstairs from the bathroom. I was annoyed that somebody had rung the front doorbell and might have inadvertently woken Victor from his nap. I was still drying my hands on a towel and preparing myself to first scold and then dismiss whoever it was, when I opened the door and saw Victor's son, Leon.

Whenever Leon responded to my infrequent text messages, he was distant yet polite, but he never initiated contact. That was part of the routine of our relationship with him—we texted, Leon occasionally replied, promises were made, and meanwhile he got on with his life and we got on with ours. Thereafter, we would wait until a birthday or Christmas gave us an excuse to once again make contact with him, after which we would fall again into our familiar silence. That said, a year or so earlier, presumably after he had served yet another spell inside, Leon did make the effort to travel to London from wherever he was now living and have a coffee with Victor in the train station. The plan had been for Victor to bring Leon back to the house, where, as agreed, I'd made lunch, but Victor called me from the station to let me know that I could turn off the oven. When he came back, Victor didn't say much, but I could tell that the visit had upset him. Text messages aside, this was the last real contact we'd had with Leon, and now here he was standing before me with a taxi pulling away over his shoulder. I quickly remembered my manners and smiled and ushered the somewhat scrawny Leon inside. He sat at the kitchen table and, as we waited for the kettle to boil, Leon stared out the window at the overgrown backyard. 'Your father will still be asleep for another hour or so, but after you've had your coffee you can go and sit quietly with him, if you like. I know he'll be happy to see your face when he opens his eyes.'

Later that afternoon, after Victor had woken up and I could hear some talking going on, I knocked gently on the bedroom door, then I went in and asked if they would mind if I took a photograph of them both. They seemed okay with it, and so I got a snap of the dutiful son sitting with his proud father. Victor's head was turned towards Leon to the extent that the trappings of his breathing apparatus would allow, and while Victor would normally have been annoyed to be asked to pose for a photograph, on this occasion he tolerated the camera. I snapped, just the once, feeling perturbed by the younger man's ungainly inward lean, and then I left them alone. That evening, the house was once again our own. Victor didn't seem to want to talk about his son, so I didn't press him. I just looked at the pain that was etched on Victor's face, for we both knew that it was almost certainly too late for him to establish any kind of real relationship with Leon.

At some point after Easter, the two of us agreed that we would make an expedition to Lorna's grave so Victor would have the opportunity to lay down some flowers. It occurred to me that Leon's visit had probably stirred some torturous feelings in Victor, but I thought it best to say nothing. The night before we were due to go to the cemetery, Victor started to talk to himself, which was not entirely unusual, but there was a new urgency to his words, plus he began to sweat, and his temperature shot up. Victor's jabbering soon began to make little sense. He looked at me and said that he had lost his home in his head, and he now felt like a traitor to himself. He blurted out, 'Ruth, they said we wouldn't survive a winter, but everything is going to be all right because we won't be staying for long.' Then Victor paused, before announcing, 'Lord, this new friendship with England doesn't please me at all.' Victor stopped, as though suddenly aware of his incoherence. He searched his mind and then returned to what he assumed was the topic on the table. 'I never imagined burying

Lorna in English soil.' At this point, I tried to encourage Victor to stop talking but he jabbed his finger at me. 'You people think that if you're polite and pretend that something isn't happening then it might just go away and not bother you again.' I calmly let Victor know that it wasn't fair to just lump me in with other people, but he continued to raise his voice. 'I try like hell to listen and know when to smile, and when to stand up for myself, but I'm too bashful for this place. Maybe my father was right when he said that I will just make a jack-arse of myself, but in all the time I'm in England I never had to resort to sleeping in a telephone box or on a park bench, and I never played the part of the grateful coloured man. I tried to be me, Ruth. Even when I wasn't sure of what I'm doing, I was always trying to hold on to some dignity. Maybe that's my mistake, that I try too hard to be dignified when I know full well that all you people see is the colour and not the man.'

By dawn, Victor had finally settled down, but I was still worried enough that I called for the doctor. By the time Dr Patel arrived, Victor was struggling to breathe, and his persistent cough was shaking his whole body in a way that now terrified me. Dr Patel reached into her pocket for her phone. Within minutes the ambulance arrived and I'm not sure how it happened, but the next thing I remember was Victor lying in the intensive care unit of the hospital and breathing more easily, while I sat on the other side of the glass window. Soon after, a young doctor I had never seen before was standing over me twiddling his pen between his fingers before carelessly dropping it to the floor. Apparently, an infection had spread, but according to the doctor all they could do at present was to stabilize Victor. Tomorrow they would run tests to determine what 'the next stage' might be (how I had grown to hate that phrase), but as of this present moment (another phrase I hated) Victor was sleeping peacefully, and it was suggested that it might be best if I went home now and got some rest. I recognized the young Polish nurse who appeared, and watched as she whispered something into the ear of the young doctor, and together they left. I made my way down to the cafeteria and tried to eat, but the most depressing part of the evening was going back to an empty house, and then making the phone call to Leon, with whom I hesitated to share the whole truth about his father's condition. I feared that Leon wouldn't care enough to make another visit, but then I did something stupid and blurted out my opinion that I thought Leon ought to come and see his father because the situation was not good. As soon as the words left my lips, I wished that I had phrased things differently. In fact, I'm still haunted by the silence that followed, for, whatever his intentions might have been, it was now clear that there was no possibility whatsoever of Leon stirring himself to make a journey to his father's bedside.

Understandably enough, I couldn't sleep that night. I lay under the covers and began to think about my mother, who I knew, were she in my shoes, would regard Victor's illness as an inconvenience that had been sent to trouble her. She was a selfish, judgmental woman who, after the summit meeting with Paul's parents about my pregnancy, showed her true colours. She waited until his parents had left before immediately labelling them as 'common', with no craving for sophistication, and clearly no desire to navigate their way into the middle classes and put some distance between themselves and National Assistance. Then she trained her sights on me, and accused me of being a trollop, and asked if I understood what 'consent' meant? For a moment I was stupefied, but she soon explained herself. 'Well, he didn't have to rape you, did he? Blow me, I never reckoned on having a slut for a daughter.' During the following weeks it soon became evident that Paul's parents must have had some words with their son, for throughout the duration of the pregnancy he was especially nice to me, sending the odd card, and sometimes calling in to see me after school, but it all felt artificially polite. Despite my hysterical pleas, after the baby was born my mother made me give Lucy up for adoption ('You don't know how to boil an egg, let alone care for a young child'). Once she did so, I started to deliberately wear clothes I was sure she would hate; skirts that were too short, or tops that were too tight, and then I left and went south. Paul wrote to me at the secretarial college, but by this time I'd begun to believe my dad's assessment of him, that he would inevitably end up as a thirty-bob-a-week layabout, and so I decided not to reply, and I never did.

Breaking contact with her birth father was another thing on the list of grievances that Lucy was ready to dump on me when I eventually reunited with her. Lucy's social worker, Mrs Moss, had written and introduced herself, and then made it clear that my young daughter had been deeply hurt by the fact that I had not replied to her letter asking if it might be possible for her to meet with me. I was shocked, and so I wrote straight back to this Mrs Moss and asked her, 'What letter?' I had never received a letter from my daughter, but yes please, I was desperate to get to know her. A few days later I got the phone call. In her la-de-da voice, Mrs Moss suggested that because Lucy was still a minor she would accompany her to London, and we might all meet in a hotel lobby and begin the process of 'repairing the past'. So, the following month, I found myself sitting alone beneath a plastic palm tree in the lobby of the King's Cross Marriott, and nervously scanning a dessert menu which threw me by including 'a salad of young vegetables' among the offerings.

Mrs Moss was tall, but her prim face looked suspiciously like that of the newly elected prime minister, Mrs Thatcher. She extended a spinsterish little hand for me to shake before turning and gesturing towards Lucy, in whose nervous features I could instantly see traces of both Paul and myself. A few minutes later the coffee arrived, and I watched my teenage daughter spoon a single heap of sugar into her drink and then stir with the stained utensil, trying all the while to disguise the fact that her hand was shaking. Mrs Moss continued to prattle. 'I explained to Lucy about your not getting the letter, but perhaps you might care to say something to her yourself about your living situation. I believe you share your life with a gentleman who, I assume, knows all about Lucy?' I nodded as the ignorant cow continued to speak. 'The next time, the pair of you will most likely be meeting without me and, as the adult, it will be your decision when to introduce your partner into the equation. However, my suggestion would be to first establish a sound platform with each other and then slowly open up your life and begin working on establishing a bond of trust.' Unfortunately, as the woman droned on, I could see scepticism writ large on my daughter's face, and it was clear that now was not the time for me to start sharing anything about Victor.

Early the next morning, I went back to the hospital and found myself sitting on a chair next to a still unconscious Victor. His lips were parted, so I could see the gaps where he had lost teeth that were simply too expensive to replace. As a result, I never liked it when Victor smiled in public, for he revealed far too much about our situation. But now it didn't matter. Danuta asked if I wanted a pad and pencil, for she said that respiratory patients sometimes preferred to write things down. I shook my head, not wanting to believe that it had come to this. I knew that if I took the kindly offered notepad I would be accepting that we were moving towards a kind of helplessness that I wasn't ready to face, and so I smiled inanely at the nurse and said nothing. The monitor occasionally beeped, and the lights flickered and danced, and for the full length of the morning Victor continued to lie in the hospital intensive care unit with one foot in each world. In the afternoon, the young pen-twiddling doctor, who seemed to have taken over from the older one, eased his way into the room and, without making eye contact, began to read to me from his clipboard notes in a flat monotone. Why, I wondered, did these doctors and nurses not understand that it's relatively simple to reassure patients and their families by just adopting a modicum of honesty and maintaining some eye contact. A straight-forward explanation of Victor's situation would have enabled me to control my anxiety, but clearly the stubble-faced youth didn't understand that he should not have been reading. He should have been looking at me and offering me a consoling smile, but the idiot continued to read from his notes. As he did so, I remembered that at some point Victor and I had managed to broach the big question of what we should do if he fell into a coma, but I couldn't quite remember the decision we had come to. Finally, the doctor looked up in my direction and began now to talk about resuscitation, before pressing on and asking about other family members. Excuse me, I thought, was I not enough? I pointed to the picture by Victor's bedside, but I said nothing. He has a son, and I have a daughter. The doctor glanced at the photograph that I had taken of Victor and Leon, and then he turned back to face me. I wanted to tell him; Victor has been here a long time. He has family, but not here. Not in England. But instead, I said, 'I think he's cold. He feels the cold. Can somebody please bring Victor another blanket? Or maybe two. And a pillow, he likes to be propped up in bed.'

After this, everything is a bit of a blur. Victor slowly improved and they decided to move him into a room by himself where Danuta, and her young doctor friend, continued to look after him. I got into the habit of visiting twice a day; first thing in the morning, and then again in the afternoon. However, Danuta was always trying to get me to stay home and rest ('I'll call you if there's any change in his situation'), but I told her that I wasn't working so it was no trouble to get on the bus and come back to the hospital. I was disappointed when the older, bald doctor started to join the younger one on the rounds, as I found him even more vexing than graceful Danuta's bumbling suitor. However, he didn't say much until the afternoon he let the West Indian sister know that he wanted to see me, and I sat before him in his office and listened as he told me that Victor could go home now. Was this a sick joke? He dismissed me without really giving me any explanation, and it was left to Danuta to point out that Victor wouldn't be able to handle stairs anymore so I might want to do something about this. Maybe move his bedroom downstairs? But a bigger problem had been slowly dawning on me for some time now. I felt ashamed to admit it, but I wasn't really sure if I wanted Victor back at the centre of my life. Why couldn't Leon look out for him now? I'd done my bit, hadn't I? Many years ago, I had decided to throw in my lot with Victor, and because of this I lost sight of Peter, a bloke who hadn't really done me any wrong. Now I had a growing sense of dread that I was in danger of losing my daughter and, each morning, I could hardly face myself in the bloody mirror. And when I did look, I didn't like what I was seeing. Then there was the Charlie bloke, who had taken to standing on the street corner trying to make me feel like a prisoner in my own home. Victor owed me a proper explanation, beyond mumbling that sometimes Charlie used to let him sleep on his bedsit floor, and he shouldn't have allowed himself to get so friendly with Charlie because 'the boy has a screw loose in his head.'

Eventually, I went in search of Peter at a jeweller's shop that unsurprisingly was no longer there, and so I took myself and my disappointment off to a pub in order that I might turn things over in my mind. I stared out the window at the hordes of people, but I was sure that the other folks in the pub were looking at me, and I could tell that I was failing to convince anyone that I was complete in my solitude. My thoughts kept fogging up. I needed to be with Lucy, at least for a short while. Surely, it was Leon's responsibility to get himself to London and look out for his father. There was no reason why he shouldn't do his bit and let me go to see my daughter and sort things out between us. As I continued to stare out the pub window it occurred to me that I might not have found Peter, but perhaps I *had* discovered a little bit of clarity. Surely, Leon should be thanking me for everything I'd done for his father over the years, instead of continually giving me the cold shoulder. And surely, what Lucy needed was, for once in her life, to feel as though I was putting her first. Once I left the pub, I made my way back to the hospital, but Victor was sleeping so I left him. On the bus home, I carefully worked out what I was going to say to Leon, and then Lucy, but no sooner had I stepped through the door and taken off my coat than the West Indian sister telephoned and said I should come back to the hospital as Victor had taken a bad turn. In the end, I never did get around to making any phone calls.

On the morning of Saturday, May 12, having spent a long night sitting by Victor's bed listening to monitors and hushed voices in the corridor, I watched Victor hatch his eyes and stare disbelievingly all about himself until his gaze finally came to rest upon me. I licked my forefinger and rubbed his lips, and watched as the words formed in his head. Once he had accumulated and ordered them, he spoke quietly. 'I want to go home.' It had clearly been a great struggle for him to deliver the short statement, but I could see that he wasn't sure if I had heard him correctly. I watched as Victor tried to summon the strength to repeat himself, but I fought back tears and whispered that he should say nothing further. I placed my hand on his arm and squeezed. Repeating himself wasn't really going to help matters.

Shortly before noon, a grouchy Danuta made an appearance, but it annoyed me that there was still no sign of either doctor. She briefly examined Victor without waking him, then looked at the machines, before asking me if I wanted to step out for some fresh air. For some reason, I felt an urge to tell Danuta that Victor used to be a journalist on a national newspaper. I wanted to go on and tell her that when things started between us, I didn't know that Victor was married. One day he told me about Lorna and his son, as though they were of no consequence, and Victor insisted that he just wanted to support Lorna until she got settled in England, that's all. He assured me that he would soon come back to me, and so I stupidly agreed to share him with her. For nearly six years, I let Victor move between his home with Lorna and Leon, and his house with me. I was stupid, because during all this time I tried hard not to think too much about the child I'd given away, for I thought that Victor wouldn't want me if I suddenly had baggage. Then, when Lucy did find me, and Victor was back living full-time with me, at least to begin with, I was too ashamed and confused to properly explain myself to my own child. But the previous lunchtime, having tried and failed to locate Peter in the heart of the City, I finally accepted that this state of unhappiness couldn't go on any longer. I had to get hold of myself before I lost my Lucy forever. Danuta continued to hover over me, and she asked again if I wanted to step out for some fresh air. I wanted to tell Danuta that at one time, Victor had been successful enough to be actually recruited by the national newspaper. And then he lost his job, and his so-called friend, Claude, was never there for him. Then Victor started to drink. Soon there was an older Victor, but the last year or two hadn't been too bad. Victor seemed to have found some peace within himself, although I still had little idea of what, if anything, I meant to this man, and this was no longer good enough. After everything I'd done for him, I felt I deserved to know, but, of course, I said none of this to Danuta, who looked entirely uninterested in whatever thoughts might be spinning through my head.

On Saturday afternoon, Victor slipped in and out of consciousness as I held on to his hand. Around teatime, a vicar entered the room unannounced, and asked if he could say a prayer. My first instinct was to tell the man to bugger off, but I held my tongue and simply stared at him. After a few moments, my withering look left the dog-collared fool in no doubt as to what I thought of him, and I watched as Mr Holy Man quickly muttered his words, and then backed out of the room and left us alone.

It is now clear to me that Victor pretty much faced every day of his illness with courage. Not a macho 'I'm going to beat this thing' kind of courage, but something much more difficult; the courage of resignation. He allowed himself to be frightened, and he occasionally let me witness his fear, which the man I first met would never have permitted me, or anyone else, to see. Somehow, I knew that Victor would enter his final sleep at night. I knew he would get the timing right, and so it proved. It was Danuta who, shortly before going off duty, once again insisted that I visit the cafeteria and get some food. She assured me the West Indian sister would keep an eye on Victor while I grabbed a snack. Sadly, I wasn't there with Victor at the end, but I understand how it must have happened. Soon after I left his room the shadows would have begun to lengthen, and Victor's breathing would have shortened. I feel sure that, in that darkened room, Victor rose up and began his journey through the tunnel towards the light. It was late spring in England, and dusk had descended. As I sat in the basement cafeteria eating my sandwich, Victor stopped breathing and stepped out of himself. He left through the window and began his journey home. And, as I always suspected he would, Victor left me behind.

7 ✐

LOSING THE LIVING

PETER EMERGED into the morning gloom from the depths of the 50th Street subway station. Once he reached the top step, he paused and held on to the cold steel banister and caught his breath. This had been his morning routine for almost ten years, but these days the steep flight of concrete steps was increasingly unkind to him. The journey on the graffiti-damaged subway train from Brighton Beach, where he rented a small first-floor room, took him nearly an hour. Among the commuters there was a shared, deathly quiet camaraderie, as though they had each taken an individual vow of silence which gave them permission to sway and nod as they saw fit, but nobody was allowed to speak. Once the train finally lumbered its way across the river to the east side of Manhattan, the passengers rose from the basement of their dreamworlds and, one by one, began to prepare themselves to meet whatever challenges the day might hold.

The walk to the apartment building where Peter worked was a short block and a half, which was just as well on this cold November morning. The leaves had fallen and were making the sidewalk mushy and treacherous for a man who was not so light on his feet. Peter's discomfort was further compounded by the fact that cold air seemed to penetrate his inadequate coat with alarming ease, but he remained hopeful that the coat might see him through the winter. As Peter drew level with the sandy limestone of his building, he checked that the adjacent sidewalk had been washed with the power hose, and that wrappers from candy bars, or swirling plastic bags, had not been allowed to remain trapped in the beds of delicate shrubbery which decorated the building's perimeter. Once he reached the front entrance, he made sure that the brass nameplate had been polished so that, as he passed by, he might glimpse an out-of-focus smudge of his own reflection, and then he scrutinized the revolving glass doors making sure that they were not disfigured by fingerprints or ugly streaks occasioned by a combination of rainfall and the grime of city life. As Peter finished his rapid inspection, he saw Ahmed standing by the desk and anxiously scanning the entrance for him. For the greater part of the night this fidgety man would have been swabbing and sweeping while keeping one eye on the door so that he might open up for those leaving early for the office or heading out to the airport to catch a morning flight.

Once Peter had carefully settled himself on the swivel

chair behind the expansive counter of the desk, he stirred the coffee powder into his cup of hot water and then picked up the heavy blood-red telephone whose only concession to modernity was the presence of push buttons instead of an old-fashioned rotary dial. After the chaos and expense incurred as a result of last year's citywide blackout, the managing agents had given up putting money into the building. As a result, the handful of staff were constantly applying inadequate Band-Aids to one problem or another, knowing full well that they would never be blessed with the funding to actually fix anything. A grumpy Ahmed had informed Peter that the elevator had broken down at around two o'clock in the morning, and it was stuck between the third and fourth floors. During the night this had simply been an inconvenience, for the residents were not the types to wander in slurring and unstable on their feet, incapable of remembering the number of their apartment. However, now that the morning rush was about to commence it was clear that a broken elevator was a serious issue.

Having barked at Peter and demanded to know what the hell kind of time this was to be calling him about 'a bullshit elevator', Mr Wickes hung up the phone. The superintendent was in Florida on a mission to buy a condo. Earlier in the year he had announced to his staff his scheme to leave the hellhole of a city to 'Son of Sam' and his friends. He was adamant that he and his asthmatic wife planned to retire and relocate to one of the beach towns an hour or so north of Miami. In Mr Wickes's absence, Peter was both doorman and temporary super, but the night doorman, Ahmed, whose official dark green jacket always hung uncomfortably about his drooping shoulders, seemed incapable of making any decision on his own. As ever, Ahmed had waited until Peter arrived before hurriedly describing the problem. Having done so, Ahmed stripped off his jacket and pulled on a hooded sweater, before bolting out into the pedestrian traffic. For a while, given the clockwork regularity of his departure, Peter had suspected that Ahmed was moonlighting as a cab driver, but the man could sometimes be a little work-shy and so Peter had decided that it was more likely that Ahmed was simply scurrying back to the room in Astoria that he shared with his brother, and quietly sleeping through the main body of the day, before appearing again in the early evening to take over from Peter.

Peter waited until eight o'clock before calling Mr Hughes in the managing agents' office. He explained the situation to him, without mentioning Mr Wickes's phone-slamming outburst, and stressed that without a working elevator many of the older folks would be trapped in their apartments for the day. He heard Mr Hughes take a hit on his cigarette and then exhale before sharing the news that the insurance company only permitted two service visits per month, and the building wasn't eligible for another visit until the end of the following week. As Peter thought quickly about how he might best impress upon this man the gravity of the situation, he noticed a reminder that yesterday afternoon he had written in bold capitals on the desk notepad. 'Rosenblatt. Hospital. Between 9 and 5.' 'Listen', said Mr Hughes with his tobacco-induced drawl, 'I tell you what. I'll give the insurance outfit a call, but I wouldn't hold your breath if I were you. These assholes ain't got an ounce of compassion about them.'

Peter put down the receiver and took a long sip of his now

lukewarm coffee. It was Mr Hughes's father who, shortly after Peter's arrival in the country, had welcomed him into the seedy offices of the managing agents, which were located on the second floor at the back of a high-rise on Flatbush. Peter noticed the two framed photographs that hung side by side on the wall behind the desk—one of Martin Luther King Jr, and the other of Robert Kennedy—and for a moment he was unsure as to whether or not he should offer his condolences. The old man lifted his glasses from his top pocket, and with an imperceptible flick of his wrist opened the frame and placed them on the bridge of his nose. He then asked Peter about his experience in the world of property management, and Peter could sense Mr Hughes looking him up and down and factoring in the lack of a wedding band, alongside the absence of any letters of recommendation, as he attempted to reach a decision. Peter tried to present himself as capable and keen, as opposed to quietly desperate, and eventually the old man leaned back in his chair, scratched his beard with the tip of a pencil, and decided to take a chance on the tubby, balding man before him. Peter started out as a swing-shift doorman in a building farther down Flatbush towards the bridge, a pretentious residence that tried to affect a kind of Manhattan sophistication with fresh flowers in the lobby, and a neon 'Taxi' sign jutting out at a right angle above the front door, although the frustrating thing wouldn't light up no matter how many times you pressed the 'call' button. When a vacancy opened in the agency's flagship Manhattan building, an eighteen-story solid structure on the east side, with a partial view of the river from the roof, Hughes senior had no hesitation in moving his most reliable employee to keep an eye on both the building and his temperamental superintendent, Louis Wickes. Five years ago, old man Hughes regrettably passed away, leaving his exasperated son with a business he clearly had little interest in. It troubled Peter that Mr Hughes junior had not yet spoken with him about the soon-to-be-vacant position of superintendent. In fact, Peter had no idea what the son's plans were for the future of the building, but he suspected they might not include him.

Peter knocked on the door of the Rosenblatt apartment, for he knew that the doorbell to #3F didn't work. Mr Rosenblatt had many times rebuffed Peter's suggestion that the handyman, Luis, come up and fix it, and so Peter had finally dropped the subject. ('Knock on the damn door, I can still hear good. I don't need no sing-song in my head.') Peter had left Luis behind the front desk, where the poor fellow would soon be absorbing caustic comments from the residents who, having reluctantly descended the spiral staircase and entered the lobby, would now be intent on letting the poor handyman know exactly what they thought of the elevator situation. Peter knocked again, and this time he heard a muffled, and resentful, 'I'm coming, dammit', followed by silence, but Peter was not concerned, for he fully understood that Mr Rosenblatt had his moods.

Rosenblatt had been one of the first to greet Peter when he initially came to work in the building. A long-term resident, Mr Rosenblatt had apparently moved in with his wife after the war, but by the time Peter began his employment in the building the midtown lawyer was a widower. However, he appeared to be a merry one, for he had a string of ladies with pearls who visited him most evenings of the week, and Peter admired how the old man kept his social world ordered. A few years ago, Rosenblatt retired from his legal practice, and Peter was surprised to realize that the well-organized man had not arranged it so that one of his lady visitors might assume a more permanent role in his life. As Rosenblatt began to develop more difficulties with walking, Peter took it upon himself to help the old curmudgeon with grocery shopping, and taking up his mail, and leaving his copy of the *Times* by his door, so that the retiree was spared the inconvenience of being seen with his walking frame. Unfortunately, the hospital appointments were a problem, for Peter worked a twelve-hour shift and therefore couldn't accompany him, so on these occasions it was Rosenblatt's nephew, a smug, self-satisfied young city financier, who reluctantly escorted his uncle. Peter knocked a third time, and once again he heard movement and then, after a short while, the chain being unhooked. The door slowly opened and, as Peter had anticipated, a slovenly and cantankerous Rosenblatt stood before him in his pajamas, with the smell of cheap American whiskey pervading the air.

Back in the lobby, Peter returned to his seat behind the desk and assured a disconsolate Luis that if Mrs Samuels in #6B buzzed down again, and insisted that somebody should walk her Pekinese, he would not be pressed into service. 'That's not your job, Luis.' The young handyman seemed relieved, and Peter continued. 'If Mrs Samuels wants somebody to walk the dog then she should call a dog-walking service.' But Peter knew that he was partly to blame for the residents' attitude, for, no matter how annoying they were, he always went out of his way to be kind to them. The impoverished Blanchards on the thirteenth floor had a pirated cable set-up that Peter had established with the engineer, who, when he came to cut them off, took the handful of crumpled notes that Peter proffered and marched straight back out to his van. Meanwhile, young Miss Tyler on the ninth floor had illegally installed a washing machine, but she was in some branch of the fashion industry, and it was clear that the young lady needed freshly laundered clothes every day. When her apartment flooded, Peter didn't report anything to Mr Wickes. He and Luis took care of the mess, and Peter persuaded the plasterer, who was working for the managing agency in the hallways, to repair the damaged ceiling in the eighth-floor apartment immediately below Miss Tyler's. He also allowed Miss Tyler to keep her washing machine.

The Samuelses on the sixth floor conveyed the impression that they had plenty of money, and they certainly had the additional bonus of each other's company, but with Mrs Samuels in particular, nothing was ever quite right. However, today Peter would have to draw the line at Mrs Samuels demanding that somebody should walk her dog simply because the elevator was out. None of the residents ever seemed curious about Peter; they never asked where he was from, or enquired where he lived, or sounded him out as to how he was feeling, but maybe he gave off the impression that people should keep their distance. Even old Rosenblatt, for whom he went out of his way on a daily basis, treated him like a paid servant. This morning, Peter reminded the pajama-clad widower that his nephew would soon be along to take him for his check-up. 'The window for the appointment is nine till five, but it shouldn't take too long.' The old man clung to his walker with balled-up fists and stared at Peter. And then Peter saw it again, the tattoo on Mr Rosenblatt's left forearm, and Peter's mind began to cloud. 'Mr Rosenblatt, I'll call you when your nephew arrives, but maybe you need to start getting yourself ready.' The old man continued to glare at him, and so Peter took a half-step back from the door. 'Mr Rosenblatt, I'll be downstairs dealing with an elevator issue, but don't you worry. When it's time we'll get you to the front door and into a car, okay?'

The nephew picked up the phone on the first ring. 'Yeah, Walter Boch here.' Peter gently reminded the insolent man that his uncle had an appointment today, and he wondered what time he might expect to see Mr Boch.

'What time? Are you serious? Who the hell are you to quiz me about my day, and get all up into my family's affairs? You're the goddamn doorman, right?'

At this moment an irate, red-faced Mr Samuels tumbled into the lobby and made straight for the desk. He was dressed in a dark blue suit and collar and tie, so Peter understood that he was on his way to Columbia University to deliver his Monday morning lecture.

'Hey, Peter, I'm not a young man and I pay a pretty hefty service charge for this place. You *are* aware of this, right?'

Peter smiled and held up one hand in the hope that Mr Samuels might understand that he was talking on the telephone.

'Mr Boch, I don't mean to get into your family's business, I just want Mr Rosenblatt to be ready when you arrive.'

But it was too late, the nephew had already hung up.

However, this now enabled Peter to turn his full attention to Mr Samuels, who was scrutinizing his watch. Luis must have heard the commotion, for he suddenly appeared in the lobby from the door that led to the machine room.

'Look, my wife is going to be stuck up there all day with the freaking dog. You know she likes to take a stroll to the East River and give the mutt a chance to you know what.'

Peter found himself nodding, but he was no longer listening to what Mr Samuels was saying. The man's mouth was moving, and Mr Samuels was gesturing with an open hand, but Peter heard nothing. Luis was staring at Peter, as though begging him to please stop this man talking and find a solution to the noisy conflict in the lobby, but Peter's mind had drifted back to Mr Rosenblatt's exposed forearm. Once Mr Samuels finally left the lobby, Peter turned to Luis and asked him to please take over on the front desk for a few minutes as he needed to step outside and take a little personal time.

Peter sat by himself in the small triangular park at the end of the block and looked at the furtive birds darting in all directions. Local volunteers tended to the garden with a ferocious devotion, protecting nascent shrubs and bushes with ingeniously crafted wire mesh cages, and posting signs everywhere about litter so that, in a way, the signs themselves had become a type of refuse. Peter remembered that long before the soldiers eventually arrived in his country, he was sure that he could hear them in their far-away land gathering up their belongings and enthusiastically slinging their rifles up and onto their shoulders. He was sure he could hear their noisy boots as they clambered into the back of their trucks. These keen soldiers were on the move—they were coming to his country. He stood in the largest of the three fields that lay behind his aunt and uncle's house and turned his head slightly so that he might better hear the commotion being lifted on the wind and billowing in his direction. A month later, Peter crouched in a ditch and actually saw the soldiers who, having effortlessly crossed the border and entered his country, seemed quietly pleased with themselves as they pulled on their cigarettes and huddled together in the back of their rowdy vehicles which rumbled ominously through the narrow country lanes.

A few weeks later, Peter found himself outside the apartment building where he used to live. He had arrived earlier in the day hoping to reconnect with his parents, but they had evidently surrendered their apartment, and their town, and their son, and taken their leave. Young Peter stood alone on the empty street and tried to come to terms with the fact that everything in his world had now changed. He stepped back into the shadows, for he feared being discovered. After all, the soldiers had left behind confident men in spotless uniforms, with black boots which reached to their knees, to ensure that the new order would be maintained. He had seen them. They were everywhere in his town. Peter looked up at the handsome building that contained his family's modest top-floor apartment, and remembered the history that his apprehensive father had shared with his worried son. According to his father's testimony, his maternal grandparents had carefully saved their money and gradually accumulated the capital which enabled them to buy the apartment and leave their fetid rented room on the end of a block of stables. They moved in and made soup; they baked bread; they created a home in this apartment for their two daughters. In the course of time, their elder daughter—a willful child and, according to Peter's father, a source of great disappointment—left the family and fled to the country and into the arms of a farmer. When their younger child, Maria, married a shy tailor, her parents cooked and cleaned, and they welcomed the new member of the family into their apartment at the top of the stairs. A grandson arrived, but the sickly elders soon departed this life and Peter grew up in the apartment with the hardship of his mother's grief and confusion sitting heavily in the air.

Peter stood in the street and turned his attention from the darkened windows and stared at the large tree in front of the building which he knew would continue to grow silently. Nobody had attempted to uproot the tree and toss it onto the back of a cart and remove it to some other place. Peter looked again at the apartment building and understood that a chain had been broken. Perhaps, in the future, might some people remember that this property was once owned, and occupied, by different residents? His aunt and uncle on the farm had warned their nephew that there would be nothing in the town for him should he return, but they were powerless to prevent him from leaving the farm. And so, this afternoon, Peter had arrived and discovered the door to the building locked. Unable to force his way inside, Peter made his way to his father's tailor shop where his father's assistant, Simon, rushed out into the street and whispered that he must leave and do so immediately. He placed a gentle hand on Peter's shoulder. 'Your parents listened and did as they were instructed: Take a blanket, food for the journey, but nothing else. All valuables, wrist watches and jewellery, are to be handed over for safekeeping. Documents too. Identification will not be necessary.' Peter instinctively understood that his proud mother would have protested her innocence, but his father would have begun his preparations, all the while asking himself why should he, a tailor, have to submit to orders from men such as these? And really, to go where? Please, tell us the truth. But his father would have asked *himself* these questions. Peter felt sure that, like all the others, his father would have marched off in a state of hopeful silence.

THERE WERE TWO ELEVATOR REPAIRMEN at work in the lobby. An excited Luis had come to find Peter in the park and let him know that the men had arrived, and they were setting about rectifying things. Instead of taking up his seat behind the desk, Peter stood beside the men, but not too close, for he was aware he occupied a lot of space. Having finished unfolding their tool kits and arranging their wrenches and hammers in the order they might be needed, the repairmen remained crouched on the ground. The door to the elevator shaft was open, and Peter felt confident enough to share his hunch with them that a cable might well have become dislodged. After all, this had been a recurring issue. The senior of the two men looked up at him.

'A cable, huh? You qualified to know about these things?'

His young colleague laughed and continued to adjust the lamp on the front of his hard helmet. Once he was satisfied, he too looked at Peter.

'Listen, Solly, or whatever your name is, why don't you

just scoot off behind your desk and let us get on with our job. This is supposed to be my day off, pal. You really think I want to be making conversation with you?'

Peter stared at the back of the man's head, unsure how to respond to this spasm of hostility. Then Bella, the Samuelses' maid, entered the lobby dressed in the unfortunate uniform that the Samuelses insisted she wear. The poor Mexican girl looked like she was somebody's possession, but without her having to say anything, Peter could see that the young maid was a bundle of nerves. He turned to Luis.

'You take the door again. I won't be long.'

Having slowly laboured his way up the stairs, Peter opened the door to the sixth floor, and he and Bella passed out of the stairwell and into the corridor. Once there, Peter could see Mrs Samuels standing by the entrance to her apartment. The woman watched as Peter shuffled somewhat breathlessly in her direction.

'Now then, Peter, don't you think it's about time you lost some weight? And maybe it's time you found yourself a lady to look after you. For heaven's sake, you're not taking care of yourself, are you?'

Peter reached the door and looked beyond Mrs Samuels and could see the three distinct piles of dog excrement on the parquet floor. Mrs Samuels continued to talk, as though this was a social visit, but Peter knew exactly why he was there and what Mrs Samuels expected.

'Perhaps the Latin boy can take care of this?'

No, he would not allow Luis to be humiliated in this way. He would take care of it himself; but he suddenly realized that he had not heard from the nephew nor, more importantly, had he heard anything from old man Rosenblatt, who could usually be relied upon to call down demanding to know what the hell was going on.

'Excuse me, Peter, where are you going?' As Peter made his way back in the direction of the stairwell, Mrs Samuels began to shout.

'Bella, go with him. Don't let that man get away. Peter, why are you being so boorish?'

But Peter didn't stop, and with the palm of his hand he pushed open the door to the stairwell and began to descend.

Rosenblatt was dead on the floor of his living room. Peter had seen dead bodies before. Many of them. He knew death when he saw it, and he immediately understood that this was not a time for hysteria. Most likely, the old man had suffered a heart attack, for he couldn't see any blood from an unexpected fall. The heart attack would have been stealthy, and it would have struck and departed before Rosenblatt had any real idea of what was happening. Peter quietly closed the door, and then used his pass-key to double lock the apartment.

Back in the lobby, the two repairmen had packed up their bags and were now busily pushing buttons and calling the car and sending it down, and then calling it up again. They were satisfied. The senior man pointed his finger at Peter as he spoke.

'You need to get your cheap-ass agency in Brooklyn to spend some money and buy a whole new system. This is a piece of junk.'

Peter squeezed behind the desk, grateful that the elevator had been fixed before the five o'clock rush. Now he would be able to greet the residents returning home from work, and act as though there had never been any kind of problem. Everything was good and it was a normal day. Peter decided that when Ahmed arrived at seven o'clock to relieve him, he would act the same way towards Ahmed. Yes, everything was good and there was no problem. The two elevator repairmen were now ready to leave, and they both approached the desk.

'Well,' said the younger one, 'like I said, it was my day off, Solly. Don't you want to tip me?' Peter knew this was unnecessary, but he was keen for the two of them to leave the building. He reached into his pants and pulled out a five-dollar bill and handed the gratuity to the younger man, who closed his fist around it before shoving the bill into his back pocket.

'Okay, be seeing you, buddy.'

Peter could see that Luis had witnessed this exchange with a discernible sense of disquiet. As they both watched the men pass through the revolving glass doors and move towards their illegally parked van, Peter thought of what he might say to Luis. But then the buzzer sounded and apartment #6B lit up on the board. Mrs Samuels. Of course, she still had an issue that needed to be dealt with.

Peter was sitting at the wooden horseshoe counter in his familiar bar, right by his subway stop in Brooklyn. As he waited for his steak to arrive, he sipped on his 'cocktail' of soda water and lime juice and stared through the huge window at people hurrying to put up their umbrellas and get home before the deluge arrived. It had already started to drizzle, and the roads were slick, and car lights were being

reflected in the shallow puddles, creating a circus-like atmosphere. Before leaving work, Peter had called the Rosenblatt
nephew, but there was no reply, so he left a message asking
the young fellow to call him in the morning any time after
seven o'clock. As Peter was readying himself to leave, he
shared with Ahmed the news that, against all the odds, the
elevator had been fixed. Ahmed received the news with
scepticism. He looked closely at Peter, as though wishing to
remind him that the elevator would almost certainly mal-
function again and, in the absence of Mr Wickes, this would,
as ever, leave them both with the problem of how to cope
with a building full of frustrated residents.

Peter heard a loud clap of thunder and turned on his stool
and looked through the window. He could now see that the
skies had opened, much as they did when, having listened to
Simon urging him to flee, Peter decided instead to go back
and, for one last time, stand outside his parents' apartment
building and stare up at the three rooms. That night he tried
to shelter from the downpour by pressing himself against the
wall, and as he did so he remembered Simon's hurried words.
His father's assistant had insisted that Peter must leave the
town, and the country, and remake himself in another place.
Go, Peter. There can be no looking over one's shoulder. The
past will offer no bridge towards a future for you. Your future
will have to be in another place and in another language. You
must draw a veil across the past and never again attempt to
peer behind it. And so, for Peter, there were never any music
lessons, nor were there any attempts by his mother to persuade
him to dance with girls. He had no parents, no childhood,

and he had no schooling. As he stared up at the apartment building, the rain continued to fall, and he tried to take Simon's words to heart. When you leave you must travel with as little luggage as possible. Please, not even memories. There must be nothing to burden the hands, or bulge the pockets, or trouble the mind. But as much as Peter wanted to please Simon, he knew what he had to do. As soon as the rain began to ease a little, and shortly after midnight, Peter stepped away from the wall and moved off in search of his parents.

Svetlana put the steak before Peter, and then spun around to get him another 'cocktail'. As she did so, Peter picked up the knife and fork and noticed the extent to which the backs of his hands were now spotted and pockmarked with dark blemishes of age. Svetlana smiled as she settled the cocktail neatly on a mat, and it once again occurred to Peter that despite her sometimes-coarse decorum, the middle-aged barmaid's skin had quite possibly once known soft cloth. However, Peter was not a man to ask questions. As he began to eat, Peter remembered that he had given away the five dollars that he had put aside for tonight's meal. Not to worry, Svetlana wouldn't make a fuss and he would explain things when she brought the check. Why, he wondered, did Mr Rosenblatt never talk about himself? He had money, he had plenty of women, but it appeared that at some point Rosenblatt had deliberately chosen to withdraw from the world and hide. Really, what kind of a life was that, sitting by yourself and listening for the sound of the fridge so that you can remind yourself that you're still alive? Suddenly the bar was kindled by a flash of lightning and the lights momentarily flickered on and off. Svetlana snorted in frustration. The jukebox would have to be reset, and two young boys with painted nails were already pestering her for their money back. Tomorrow, Peter would make sure that Mr Rosenblatt made a dignified exit out of the building. How, exactly, he wasn't sure, but he wasn't going to allow Rosenblatt to be pushed out the back door and into the alleyway, which is where the removal trucks and ambulances generally pulled up. Mr Rosenblatt was going out the front of the building. Peter was the day doorman. He was going to make sure of it.

8 ✑

THE JOURNEY HOME

VICTOR WAS LYING IN BED with his eyes closed and his body turned towards the wall. His knees were slightly drawn. He knew that it was Saturday evening. The noises in the hospital were different on the weekend, particularly so towards the end of the day. They were less frantic and lacked any urgency. However, there was something pressing about the pain that continued to torment him, but he didn't want to trouble Ruth and repeat his complaints. After all, despite yesterday's surprising announcement that she wished to spend some time with her daughter, Ruth had been good enough to sit with him all night, and she had remained with him throughout this seemingly endless Saturday. Given the absence of the young doctor, it was she alone who had offered him comforting words of reassurance and tried to keep his spirits up. He could now hear Ruth speaking in a hushed whisper to the Polish nurse, but the woman lacked Ruth's good manners, and was making little attempt to modify her voice or rein in her foul mood. Ruth continued to calmly state her concerns until the nurse once again interrupted her.

'He says he wants to go where?' The nurse's inflection betrayed exasperation. 'Listen, they all say strange things, but they're just frightened. It's normal.'

Victor listened as the woman attempted to change the direction of the conversation.

'Come on, Ruth. Take yourself down to the cafeteria. You need to eat.'

'I'll be fine.'

'I'm off duty soon and I want to know that you've eaten.'

After a momentary pause, he heard a resigned Ruth sigh, and he listened to the slight scuffling commotion as she stood up from the plastic chair.

Victor waited a few moments until he was sure that Ruth had left for the cafeteria. Only then did he carefully turn his body in the direction of the room and open his eyes. He asked the lithe Polish nurse for some water and watched as the woman placed one hand on her hip.

'I can get you some water, but maybe you will have to wait a moment.'

Victor nodded, for he no longer had the energy to argue with this nurse.

'And please, no more with your carrying on and asking for Ruth. She won't be long. She deserves a rest, don't you think?'

With this said, the aggravating woman left the room without waiting for a reply.

YESTERDAY MORNING, Victor had tossed and turned while waiting for Ruth to arrive. However, by nine o'clock he accepted that something must have happened, and so he closed his eyes and tried to go back to sleep. It was then that he heard the confusion in the doorway to his room, as the incensed nurse began to berate the young doctor. 'You think you can just use me and then go back to your wife, is that it?' Every time the doctor tried to speak, the nurse cut him off in an increasingly aggressive fashion, and their confrontation began to grow in volume. Victor wasn't stupid; he had noticed the sideways glances between them, and overheard their childish giggling, and he had suspected that some courtship was going on between the two of them, but it was none of his business. Victor opened his eyes and saw the young doctor shaking his head as he edged away from the door. The nurse turned and looked angrily at Victor, as though about to deliver some admonishment, but she thought better of it and rushed out into the corridor in pursuit of the fleeing man.

Early yesterday afternoon, Ruth finally arrived at the hospital, but Victor could see on her face that something had changed. However, before he had a chance to tell her about the morning's drama, Ruth announced that she was going to get in touch with Leon. 'I think it will be good for you to spend some time with your son.' Victor listened without quite understanding what she was trying to say. His palm remained open, but he noticed that Ruth had not yet dropped her hand into his. 'Victor, I'm sorry, but I've made a terrible mistake. I need to spend some time with Lucy.' He repeated her words. 'You need to spend some time with Lucy?' Only now did Ruth lower her hand into his, but she chose not to grip. They sat together, limp hand in limp hand, for the best part of the afternoon without either one of them offering up any more words, until Ruth whispered that she should probably go back to the house and have an early night. Victor nodded. He had tried, and failed, to move past his feeling that Ruth was in the process of abandoning him, but he sensed that she was not ready for the strain of any further conversation and so he chose to say nothing.

Soon after Ruth's awkward departure, the West Indian sister came on duty, and she could see that Victor remained in considerable discomfort. She encouraged him to rest, and then turned on her rubber soles and left the room so that her patient might have some privacy. But both Victor's mind and his body were now under permanent siege, and so he called for the sister's help. Having listened patiently to him, the sister excused herself, and Victor eavesdropped as the woman picked up the telephone and made a call to Ruth, asking her to return to the hospital. Having done so, he saw the woman adjusting her bob of brown hair, before coming to sit quietly with him, and together they waited for Ruth to arrive. Victor looked at the sister, who, for a moment, reminded him of his long-suffering mother, and then he squinted, for he was now having difficulty maintaining focus. Suddenly, he saw his father peering at him. The man was looking closely at the fountain pen that stood in the top pocket of Victor's shirt. Victor remembered that he had just told his father that he had saved enough money to buy a passage to England, but the older man pointed a finger and asked him, 'You ever hear of a coloured man able to feed himself with a pen?' Then his father started to laugh.

On Saturday morning, the sister smiled in the direction of a clearly exhausted Ruth, who had sat with Victor through a long and turbulent Friday night. She then announced that she was giving Victor a sedative that she hoped might enable him to sleep for the day. The sister gently touched Victor's forehead with the back of her hand, checking to make sure that he didn't have a fever.

'Mr Victor, all night you keep asking me to get you a ticket to go home, but where am I supposed to get that kind of money, eh? Listen to me, stop it with your nonsense and get some rest.'

She chuckled, then reassured Ruth that the young doctor would soon be arriving, and before she went off duty she would leave a note, letting him know that he should immediately check in with Victor.

'The doctor?' Victor's voice was faint, and he spoke without opening his eyes. 'You talking about the Polish girl's friend?'

'Now then, Mr Victor, we don't need that kind of good-for-nothing chat.'

'That girl scares the poor man to death.'

The sister laughed quietly to herself. 'Mr Victor, behave yourself, you hear?'

The woman smiled at Ruth as she left the two of them alone.

NOW THAT IT WAS SATURDAY EVENING, the West Indian sister was back on duty, and it was she, not the ill-tempered nurse, who finally brought him the water. The sister stood over Victor and set the glass on the table to the side of the bed. She then rolled the machinery a little closer to Victor's bedside and began to make some adjustments to the morphine drip. Victor opened his mouth to ask the sister a question but, at the end of a long, sleepless day, he felt too depleted to deliver the words. The woman removed her horn-rimmed spectacles, cleaned them with a tissue, then replaced them on the end of her nose. She looked again at the read-out from one of the monitors.

'Mr Victor, if it's your wife you're looking for, she's downstairs in the cafeteria.'

Victor leaned over, exerted himself to pick up the glass of water, and took a tiny sip.

'Let me ask you a question. Mr Victor, you have anybody else in your life? I mean, your wife is kind to you, everybody can see that, but she has her own people. I don't mean to get in your private matters, Mr Victor, but you here in this country all by yourself?'

The sister continued to fiddle with the machinery, but Victor heard the question echoing around his weary mind. The words distressed him, so he fixed his gaze on the lumpy formations beneath the sheet that he knew were his feet. He hoped that the sister might realize that, although he had no desire to be rude, the pain had once again become unbearable, and it was difficult for him to speak. As he had anticipated, the doctor had failed to visit with him today, and so his suffering was compounded by a troubling suspicion that he was being neglected.

Some minutes later, the West Indian sister finished tinkering with the equipment and without questioning him any further she left his room. Victor took another small sip of water and then reached for the cable and pressed the red button. He immediately felt some relief, so he waited a short while and then pressed a second time, and once again he felt a surge of comfort, although he understood that on this occasion there should have been no delivery of medicine. The respite was temporary, and the sister's question continued to torment Victor. ('You here in this country all by yourself?') He waited a few minutes before eventually mustering enough force to squeeze the button a third time, and then his listless hand fell, and almost immediately his mind was illuminated with a succession of perplexing images which flickered into view. Victor saw Billy, whose face was bruised. After the night on deck with the captain, the frightened boy refused to come up and talk with him anymore. He saw young Charlie, with whom he had, out of politeness, occasionally shared a late-night drink. However, it was only after the strangely intense young man let Victor sleep on the floor of his bedsit that Charlie confessed he liked coloured men, and he tried clumsily to touch Victor. Then Victor felt ashamed to see himself furtively stealing small amounts of cash from behind the bar in the Notting Hill pub, but how else was he going to bring Lorna and the boy over to England? To this end, he also started to thief a few pounds here and there from Mr Peter's tenants, and he would tell the foreign man that the damn people hadn't paid all of their rent. He saw Mr Peter smiling at him and indulging his rent collector by pretending that he believed loyal Victor. 'Let's be kind and forgive them this time.' Victor saw himself in the hallway of Ruth's house, squatting to pick up letters from the doormat. He noticed an envelope that was marked with a return address to a 'Lucy'. Realizing that this must be Ruth's daughter, he quickly stuffed the envelope into his pocket. Later in the day, Victor ripped up the letter and threw it in a dustbin, for the idea of sharing Ruth with anybody frightened him. Then he saw himself seated at a small circular table near the entrance to a railway platform. When his frustrated son told him that he had been no kind of father to him, and got to his feet and departed, it was then that the tears began to flow. The full measure of what he had lost in England was now clear. Suddenly, this image stopped flickering, and he was forced to stare hard at a picture of a desolate man who, because he had lost a child, had essentially lost himself. By the time Victor rose from the circular table, and wiped away his tears, it was dark outside. He made his way home to Ruth, who looked at him sympathetically, and then held both of his hands in hers, for she recognized somebody else who was also failing in their battle to combat loneliness. So too was the woman on the back seat of the bus, who had managed to fall asleep with her head against the vibrating glass. Victor was haunted by the appearance of this lonely, sleeping woman, but then a smile unexpectedly touched his lips, for he was now confronted with the image of his young self under a bridge. On the first night that Lorna waited for him, Victor brought her a bunch of red poinsettias and some peanuts twisted into a piece of brown paper, and she looked at him and with a gap-toothed grin said, 'I like flower, Victor', and Victor instinctively fought back the urge to correct the fifteen-year-old girl's grammar. He knew she was clever, and it really didn't matter to him that she had a country accent. And then again, she spoke. 'Victor, I like flower.' He drew an idle line in the dirt with the outside of his shoe, before he heard himself whisper, 'I'm glad.' A thin smile appeared on Victor's face, for finally he was back home, with Lorna, and then a high-pitched note of alarm split the hospital air, but nobody rushed to Victor's side. The young doctor had clearly taken the day off, and the nurse would not be back on duty until Sunday morning. His Ruth was sitting alone in the cafeteria and, having given her patient the gift of a ticket home, the West Indian sister was standing sentry at the door. It was time. Victor understood that, having finally broken clear of the pain, he was now free to leave.